Fire For Effect
A Recon Diaries Story

This is a work of fiction. Similarities to real people, places, or events are entirely coincidental.

FIRE FOR EFFECT

First edition. November 11, 2024.

Copyright © 2024 Kendall McKenna.

ISBN: 979-8227895219

Written by Kendall McKenna.

Chapter 1

Kellan climbed out of the Town Car and glanced around at the hotel. It was finished and landscaped like an old Spanish Villa, very much in keeping with the flavor of Santa Barbara. Blossoming trees and shrubbery were in abundance all around the property. Colorful flowers were woven into trellises and iron work. Kellan inhaled deeply, his body and mind immediately recognizing the moist, salty scent of the ocean. The sun was warm on his face, the heat mitigated by the cool breeze.

It had never quite felt like home, but some of Kellan's most formative years had taken place in Southern California. Much of the training and the learning he'd done that had made him an officer, a leader and a man had taken place on, or often right in, the Pacific Ocean. Those memories tightened Kellan's chest.

He shook himself from his reverie when a bellhop came forward, pushing a luggage cart, and began to assist the driver with retrieving Kellan's luggage from the trunk.

"Good afternoon, sir," the handsome, tanned young man greeted. "Checking in?"

"Yes, I am," Kellan replied, slinging the strap of his laptop bag over his shoulder.

"Welcome to the Inn of the Spanish Garden." The young man had a gorgeous smile.

"Thank you," Kellan replied distractedly as he tipped the car driver. He'd pre-paid for the transport when he'd booked it.

"Are you staying with us long?" The bellhop pushed the cart holding Kellan's single, large suitcase toward the hotel entrance.

"Five days." That was all the leave Jonah could get, for operational reasons.

"Business or pleasure?" The young man continued with the typical polite small talk.

"A little of both," answered Kellan. "I'm participating in a symposium at UCLA and touring some of the local Navy bases. Afterward, I'm taking a few days to relax."

"Is this your first time in California?" They crossed the lobby toward the registration desk.

"No. I was stationed at Camp Pendleton for four years." Kellan withdrew his wallet from his laptop bag.

"You're a civilian now? Where did you fly in from?" The young man's interest seemed genuine.

"Yes, I'm a civilian working in D.C. now." The small pang of loss surprised him, even after all these years. Once a Marine, always a Marine.

"Well, welcome back, sir." The bellhop gestured toward the registration desk. "They'll get you checked in right over there. I'll wait here to take you up once you have your keys."

"Thank you." Kellan gave the man a small smile. He didn't need help with one fucking suitcase. But like Jonah kept telling him, he had an influential job now and should act like the VIP he was becoming.

The young woman at the registration desk was quick and efficient. She gave him a fast run down of the hotel amenities before sliding two key cards into a paper sleeve and pushing them across the counter toward Kellan.

"Enjoy your stay, Mr. Reynolds, and please don't hesitate to let us know if we can help you with anything." She was perfectly professional but her demeanor still held a note of flirtation.

Kellan tipped the bellhop well before closing the door behind him. The young man was very solicitous and seemed eager to please. It wasn't his fault Kellan desperately wanted to be alone so that he could make a phone call.

"Are you all checked in?" Jonah asked in greeting.

"Checked in and waiting for you," Kellan replied, starting to unpack for his stay. He gave Jonah his room number and brief directions to the room, once he arrived at the hotel.

"I'm nearly there," said Jonah. "I still say I should have picked you up at the airport."

"You know how unpredictable L.A. traffic is," Kellan reminded him. "I didn't want us to be stressed out over me having to cool my heels at the airport if you got delayed."

"I wouldn't have let that happen," Jonah said firmly and Kellan nearly believed he had control of Los Angeles freeways.

"I'll see you when you get here," Kellan said with a chuckle and they ended the call. His heart raced and his stomach knotted pleasantly.

Kellan turned on the television for the background noise and finished hanging his clothes. When he'd laid out his toiletries in the luxurious bathroom, complete with soaking tub, Kellan checked his email on his phone. There was nothing that required his immediate attention, since the workday on the east coast was over.

He smiled to himself as he admired the fireplace in the small sitting area. Kellan pushed open the French doors that led to the private balcony that overlooked the swimming pool and tiled fire pit. With the exception of the symposium and base tours, he didn't expect they would be leaving the room very often in the next five days.

Especially once Jonah got a look at the four-poster Queen Anne bed that was the centerpiece of the gorgeous room.

A loud knock sounded at the door and Kellan's heart leapt.

He pulled the balcony doors closed behind himself, fumbled with the TV remote, and nearly ran across the room to the door. Kellan tugged the door open and stood frozen. It had been six months since he'd seen Jonah. Six months since Jonah's TAD had been terminated and he'd been ordered to return to 1st Recon at Camp Pendleton. Six months had passed since Kellan had been able to feel Jonah's skin, smell his scent, and make love with him.

"Hey," he greeted casually, drinking in the sight of Jonah standing, tall and lean, in the corridor. "Did you find it all right?"

"Yeah, no problem," Jonah replied, as if they'd seen one another just last week.

Kellan couldn't catch his breath. He hastily stepped aside to let Jonah enter the room. Languorously, Jonah crossed the threshold, a well-stuffed rucksack slung over his shoulder. Kellan noticed that Jonah had regained his tan. The clothing he wore; board shorts, tank top and flip-flops, made him look like the California surfer he was. Kellan's palms itched with urge to touch.

Securing the door, Kellan followed Jonah into the room. Jonah set his ruck on the floor at the foot of the bed. He took in his surroundings with a critical expression that was so typical of Jonah. "Not bad," he remarked, turning slowly in a circle.

"I left you space in the bureau and the closet if you want to unpack," Kellan said as he leaned against the tall post of the bed. He was strangely hesitant to approach Jonah, at the same time he savored the anticipation.

"I'll get to that later," replied Jonah. "There's a couple of things I want to do first." He faced Kellan, standing tall and meeting Kellan's gaze directly.

Jonah's blue eyes were hungry. His lips parted and his chest heave with each ragged breath. There was tension in every line of his frame and Kellan could sense his anticipation.

Wetting his own lips, Kellan pushed off the bed post and slowly closed the few feet of distance that separated him from the heat of Jonah's body. His face flushed, his cock pushed against the front of his jeans and continued to grow harder. Kellan ached to touch and to taste Jonah.

"Oh yeah?" Kellan's voice sounded husky to his own ears. "Anything you need my help with?" He looked up into Jonah's eyes, unblinking.

"If you don't mind." Jonah's voice was rough and barely audible.

Kellan caved first but he didn't give a fuck anymore. He slid his arms over Jonah's shoulders, pressed himself to the length of Jonah's body. Kellan covered Jonah's mouth with his own, pushing his tongue inward; demanding entrance, not asking.

Jonah's arms came around Kellan's back and gripped his ass firmly. Jonah's hardness pushed against his own and he rubbed himself against it. Pulling back on a gasp, Jonah breathed harshly against Kellan's cheek. Each exhalation was rapid and hot.

"I missed you," Kellan said, voice strangled. "God, how I have fucking missed you."

"I'm glad you did," Jonah murmured against Kellan's throat. "I was afraid I was the only one." His hands pulled impatiently on the hem of Kellan's short sleeved Henley.

Kellan stripped Jonah of his tank top. As soon as Jonah's shirt was off, Kellan pulled Jonah back against him roughly. He licked at Jonah's mouth, nipped at his lower lip, and enjoyed the press of their naked chests together. Jonah's skin was warm, the light sprinkling of hair was coarse against Kellan's nipples and made them tingle.

Jonah pushed Kellan backward into the bedpost. Kellan made a sound of protest against Jonah's tongue. He shoved at Jonah's shoulders, creating enough space between them so that Kellan could drop to his knees.

Kellan impatiently pushed Jonah's hands out of the way, eager to open the Velcro fastenings of his board shorts. Jonah kicked off his flip-flops, stepped out of his shorts, and pushed everything out of their way with one foot.

He was more gorgeous than Kellan remembered, and he'd thought his memory was pretty fucking vivid. Jonah sucked a harsh breath in through his teeth when Kellan grasped the base of his cock. The curls that tickled Kellan's fingers were just a few shades darker than Jonah's high and tight hair cut. Jonah's erection stood proudly, the dusky red tip just beginning to weep pre-come.

Kellan wet his lips and looked up the length of Jonah's body, seeking his gaze. Jonah stood rigidly, hands fisted at his sides. His face and chest were flushed, his blue eyes luminous as he stared down hungrily at Kellan. His red lips were parted and he breathed through them harshly, his chest rising and falling rapidly. Kellan smoothed his free hand up Jonah's taut, defined belly. Jonah exhaled explosively, covering Kellan's hand with one of his own.

Wetting his lips again, Kellan pooled his spit. He opened his mouth and took the head of Jonah's cock inside. Kellan sucked at the hardened flesh, sliding forward, dragging the flat of his tongue down the underside of Jonah's shaft.

Jonah's free hand gripped the bedpost over Kellan's head with a loud slap. His hand that gripped Kellan's tightened convulsively. "Oh shit, Kel," Jonah sobbed hoarsely.

Kellan looked up into Jonah's eyes again. Jonah stared town at him intently. A small frown appeared between his brows, as if he was concentrating on controlling his body's reactions. Jonah's mouth hung open slightly as he breathed heavily. Kellan wanted to shatter Jonah's legendary self-control.

Pushing his mouth toward the base of Jonah's cock, Kellan took him as far down his throat as he could. He paused, breathing steadily through his nose. The musky scent of Jonah's pubic hair made Kellan's dick twitch and push against the front of his jeans. He pulled off slowly, leaving Jonah's shaft shiny and wet.

The hand Jonah used to grasp Kellan's released him abruptly, sliding into Kellan's hair and gripping the back of his head. Kellan felt Jonah's fingers clench reflexively, as if he was struggling not to drag Kellan's head forward. Kellan smiled around the width of Jonah's cock.

Using both hands to grip Jonah's hips, Kellan steadied Jonah. When Kellan found his rhythm, he slid his hands around to grasp Jonah's ass cheeks. Kellan pulled Jonah forward, pushing the head of his cock further down his own throat. Easing back, Kellan guided Jonah's hips backward, until his erection nearly slid from between Kellan's lips. He sucked Jonah's dick down again, pushing firmly with his tongue to increase the pressure and the friction.

"Kellan," Jonah cried out. It was partly desperate and almost entirely affectionate. "It's been too long, I can't hold back. Is this how you want it?"

Kellan's head spun with his victory and his cock throbbed with a fresh rush of blood. He pulled off of Jonah's erection with a loud, wet gasp. "Maybe later," he rasped.

As Kellan climbed to his feet, Jonah tugged him up and dragged him into his arms. Kellan wrapped his arms around Jonah's torso and opened his mouth eagerly for the hot, wet, hard kiss. His stomach clenched and fluttered when Jonah's fingers tickled him as they struggled with the button of his jeans.

Kellan's impatience got the better of him. He pivoted his hips, nudging Jonah toward the bed. Jonah resisted, refusing to fall backward when his legs contacted the mattress.

"I want you naked with me," Jonah demanded, his fingers again getting in Kellan's way.

Kellan's cock ached as he finally managed to get his fly open. "I'm trying," he said against Jonah's mouth. "Now just get on the bed."

At last, Jonah capitulated, lying back against the plump pillows stacked against the headboard. He looked hungry and impatient for Kellan to debauch him. Kellan toed off his Vans and kicked them aside. Hurriedly, he pushed his jeans down his legs and stepped out of them. Climbing onto the bed, he straddled Jonah's hips.

Kellan rocked back and forth, watching Jonah's expression, enjoying the play of emotion and sensation across his face. Kellan circled his hips, Jonah's cock rubbing against his ball sac and sliding against his hard cock. Jonah's skin was warm against Kellan's thighs, his muscles firm as he pushed upward rhythmically. When his cock dragged against the length of Jonah's, Kellan shuddered.

Jonah sat up abruptly, wrapping his arms around Kellan's torso and pulling him down. Kellan breathed harshly through his nose as Jonah kissed him relentlessly. Jonah's tongue was rough and demanding, sweeping through Kellan's mouth and over his teeth.

Kellan pushed out of Jonah's arms, breaking their kiss with a loud, wet smack. Jonah grabbed for him, making a frustrated sound low in his chest.

"I can't wait," Kellan said angrily. He'd wanted to drag this out, make it last. He'd wanted to drive them both insane with need before they consummated their reunion but he had to have Jonah now.

Kellan dragged open the drawer of the bedside table. He withdrew a large bottle of lubricant. They'd gotten tests and results six months after they'd both gotten back from Iraq and condoms were a thing of the past for them.

Jonah hissed when Kellan covered the head of his cock with lube. Kellan spread the viscous liquid down the shaft.

"Wait," Jonah gasped, "are you sure?"

"Yeah," Kellan replied breathlessly. "Are you?"

"If it's what you want." Jonah's body strained against Kellan's.

Coating his fingers with lube, Kellan reached between his own legs. Jonah groaned, his eyes going wide. Kellan pushed his slick fingers into his ass, coating his inner walls. Shifting position, Kellan lined up the head of Jonah's cock with his own clenched opening.

He braced his free hand against Jonah's chest. With his other, Kellan held Jonah's erection against his asshole. His thighs trembled slightly. "Hold me steady, Jonah," he whispered, his body aching to be filled.

Jonah's broad, strong hands spanned Kellan's ribs and steadied him. Kellan pushed himself downward, taking Jonah's cock into his body. He cried out loudly as the abrupt breach of his hole sent a frission racing up his spine. Kellan braced both hands against Jonah's chest and rose up slightly before he sank down again, taking Jonah's dick even deeper.

Euphoria washed over Kellan when he finally had Jonah all the way inside. When his ass cheeks pressed to the tops of Jonah's thighs, Kellan stopped moving. He waited for his body to adjust to the invasion and the stretch. With each breath, he moaned in pleasure.

"Fuck, Kel," Jonah growled. "You okay?" His hands on Kellan's ribcage trembled.

Kellan gave a sharp nod. He bit down on his lower lip and started to move. Adjusting his grip and his angle, Kellan wrapped his hands around Jonah's biceps. He moved up and down, taking Jonah deep. He rocked back and forth, grinding against Jonah and getting just a teasing hint of pressure against his sweet spot.

Gooseflesh rose on Kellan's skin. His blood roared in his ears, he panted, and his erection swayed heavily as he rode Jonah's hard cock. Kellan watched Jonah watching him as they moved against each other. The room filled with low pitched grunts and masculine groans. Sweat broke out along Kellan's hairline and it slicked their skin so they slid sensuously against each other.

Fuck, Kellan had missed Jonah. After a five year separation, they'd had nearly two years together before Jonah had been ordered to return to Camp Pendleton. They'd spent the last six months clear across the country from each other, with Jonah unable to get leave and Kellan still catching up on long neglected projects.

Jonah startled Kellan by moving quickly. He grabbed Kellan's forearms and tugged him down. Kellan toppled forward onto Jonah, palms skidding along the comforter.

"You're too far away up there," Jonah said roughly. "I can't feel you against me."

Kellan's chest was wrapped in the steel band of Jonah's arm, his head cradled in the palm of Jonah's hand. When he moved, Jonah's body slid against Kellan's sensitive cock, sending a jolt rocketing up

Kellan's spine. Kellan moaned into Jonah's hot mouth, rubbing his tongue against Jonah's aggressive one.

Jonah's fingers tightened in Kellan's hair and yanked his head backward, breaking the kiss. Kellan cried out, Jonah's mouth hot and wet on his throat.

"Oh fuck, Jonah," Kellan said, voice torn.

Kellan was held tight against Jonah's body. He clutched at Jonah's shoulders, his cock pressed between their bodies and rubbing against both of their bellies. Kellan didn't have leverage to move like he had been. Instead, Jonah took over, snapping his hips upward. His dick slid deep inside of Kellan, stretching his rim. The power of his thrusts tore broken cries from Kellan's throat.

"Feels so good to be inside you again," Jonah whispered brokenly, keeping his face pressed tightly to Kellan's throat.

Kellan wished Jonah didn't still need to hide when he told Kellan what he was feeling. At least he could feel it in Jonah's every touch. Sparks scattered behind Kellan's eyelids each time Jonah's cock slid deep inside of him. Their sweat-slick bellies stroked Kellan's rigid, sensitive cock.

"Jonah, Jonah, Jonah," Kellan chanted in a harsh whisper. His body vibrated as his orgasm built momentum. He was trapped between wanting Jonah's cock deeper and needing more friction on his own straining erection. Kellan's fingers tightened reflexively on Jonah's shoulders as a thunderstorm raged through his body. "Fuck, Jonah, like that, don't stop. Don't fucking stop."

Kellan's body tightened and he couldn't move. His spine bowed as he lay atop Jonah, his ass clenching tight around Jonah's cock. He was joyously helpless as Jonah fucked up into him, forcing wave after wave of his climax out of him. Kellan's balls ached, his dick throbbed as hot come pooled between their bodies.

"Christ, your ass is so tight around me," Jonah murmured as he held Kellan's shuddering body. "I love to feel you come against me, feel you in my arms as you come."

Even as Kellan's orgasm eased its hold on his body, Jonah's slammed into him. Kellan was pinned against Jonah's heated body as he quaked and gasped. Jonah's cock pulsed deep inside of Kellan's ass. Hot jets of come coated Kellan's inner walls, filling him and heating him at his core. Jonah chanted mindlessly against Kellan's neck, his breath hot and moist.

When Jonah collapsed against the bed, boneless, Kellan relaxed down on top of him. He knew he should move. He could smell their sweat and his own come, knew it was drying tacky between them. Jonah's cock was softening, beginning to slide from Kellan's ass, his jizz leaking out. Kellan simply couldn't get his muscles to move.

Beneath him, Jonah's chest heaved with each harsh breath. Kellan's matched Jonah's, as they lay pressed together. He really should get up and get them clean.

• • • •

KELLAN WENT TO ANSWER the knock at the hotel room door. He glanced around once more to make sure it wasn't glaringly obvious two men were staying a hotel room with a single bed. Not that it really mattered, but like Jonah said, why flaunt it?

He tipped the middle-aged man who wheeled in the cart and left it by the sliding glass door. When Kellan glanced out to the terrace again, Jonah was comfortably reclined on a chaise lounge, eyes closed. Kellan wouldn't mind a nap but he needed food first.

Jonah set a low table between two deck chairs placed facing each other. Kellan uncovered all the food dishes and unwrapped the utensils. Together they carried full plates onto the terrace and settled in to eat.

Before Kellan could take a bite, Jonah offered him a strawberry from his own plate. Kellan's pulse fluttered as he took the offered fruit from Jonah's fingers, chewing slowly. Jonah surprised him by leaning across the small table to place a soft kiss on Kellan's mouth. When he drew back, Jonah's expression was warm and affectionate. Kellan enjoyed this gentler side of Jonah.

"So, I optioned for First Sergeant in my latest fit-rep," Jonah said without preamble.

Kellan stared at him for several moments, trying to gauge what the declaration really meant. He wasn't quite ready to let himself hope. "Is that because you want to?" he asked carefully. "Or did I pressure you? Because that wasn't my intention."

"No, I never felt pressured," Jonah reassured quickly. "You gave me a lot to think about and consider, that I might not have otherwise."

"Master Sergeant is a very valid career path," Kellan said, needing Jonah to be sure. Needing Jonah to say the words.

"I realized you had a good point. I've proven my skills and leadership abilities in combat and technical billets." Jonah paused to take a swallow of beer, looking out over the pool, not meeting Kellan's eyes. "It would probably be pretty easy for me to make Master Gunny, but it'll be a challenge to make Sergeant Major."

"But when you do, you'll be a well rounded Sergeant Major," Kellan said with a smile, pride swelling in his chest. Jonah was exactly the kind of Marine who could, and would, make it through the entire ranks of Senior NCOs before he retired.

Before Jonah could utter the snide remark Kellan knew he was formulating, Kellan pressed a red grape to his lips. Jonah took the fruit into his mouth along with Kellan's thumb. He sucked gently and Kellan shivered in response.

"So, will you hear about the first round of promotions in time for the next First Sergeant's class?" Kellan asked casually. The class was held in Quantico and would give them two weeks to be close to each other. Maybe more if Jonah wanted to take leave. Kellan was never sure, Jonah seemed so indifferent at times.

"I should, yeah," Jonah replied and Kellan wondered if he detected eagerness. "Once I complete that course, I'm eligible for the five weeks of SEPME." The corner of Jonah's mouth quirked in a small smile.

"Good." Kellan returned his grin. "I'm trying to line up as many speaking engagements on the west coast as possible."

"I could make it easy and just take orders at Quantico or somewhere in DC." Again, Jonah looked everywhere but at Kellan.

"But you love California," Kellan blurted, frowning. It almost sounded as though Jonah was offering more than Kellan had expected.

"No, I *like* California," Jonah replied, pushing food around his plate. "I love *you*."

Kellan stopped breathing, his blood thundered in his ears. His grip on his fork turned his knuckles white. "Good," he said breathlessly. "I love you, too. But I don't expect you to make career decisions to accommodate me."

"I know, and that's probably one of the reasons I want to do it," Jonah said quietly. "Think about it, though; I've got a career that offers a lot of opportunity in multiple locations. You need to be in DC to do your job. It makes sense for me to move."

When Jonah finally met his eyes, Kellan saw a myriad of emotions, none of which was indifference. "It would make me very happy to have you close by, but I don't expect or demand it."

"What if I'd be doing it for myself?" Jonah asked with just an edge of annoyance. "This last six months have sucked," he said vehemently.

Kellan knew when to let something go. Jonah had made his decision and Kellan was convinced he'd made choices he would be happy with. That Kellan was lightheaded with joy as well, was just a side benefit.

Clearing his throat awkwardly, Kellan changed the subject. "How are the guys of First Recon?"

Jonah lifted a shoulder negligently. "Same badass door kickers as always, just getting younger every year."

Kellan chuckled. "How is Corporal Yarwood doing?"

Jonah brightened when he answered. "Much better. It's like having the old Corey back."

"I'm glad to hear that." Kellan meant that. He'd liked Corporal Yarwood when he'd met him in Iraq, only Corey had been a Private back then. When all the facts had been compiled regarding the events surrounding Kellan's abduction, both he and Jonah had been surprised to learn just how heroic Corey had been, despite a concussion. "You've demonstrated an extraordinary level of leadership in helping him overcome his difficulties."

"I don't know how true that is," Jonah said dubiously.

"Leadership is about more than issuing orders and administering discipline," Kellan reminded him. "Did he ever confide in you?"

Jonah sighed heavily. "It's the age old story of being dumped by a Suzy Rottencrotch."

There was something in Jonah's tone that told Kellan there was more to the story. "And?"

"Corey has rebounded in the arms of strange men," Jonah replied, completely expressionless.

Kellan narrowed his eyes as he regarded Jonah. He realized he wasn't surprised. "Is he in denial?"

"Not at all," Jonah said with a shake of his head. "But his family is, and I think drinking dulls the pain of their disapproval."

"Poor kid," Kellan sighed.

"He's going to be okay, I think," Jonah replied. "It didn't get in the way of his making Corporal, and it seems the promotion woke him up to reality. He's been doing really well lately."

"Good. I'm glad to hear that." A sense of peace settled over Kellan that he hadn't felt since before he'd met Jonah for the first time.

Jonah cleaned up the remnants of their meal and brought Kellan another beer. He sank down into his chair with a deep sigh.

"They're sending a car for me in the morning," Kellan blurted, unable to find a way to ease into the topic.

Jonah nodded but said nothing.

"You're welcome to ride with me, or drive yourself," he persisted. "I don't know how open you want to be about us."

"You know I hate hiding," Jonah said impatiently. "I like my privacy; I don't ever flaunt anything about my personal life. But it feels wrong to pretend I'm something I'm not. It's inconvenient to avoid doing something I wouldn't think twice about if I was straight."

"You know how I feel about it," Kellan replied. "But I'm not likely to be beaten, killed, or discharged if someone connects the dots."

"Realistically, neither am I," Jonah mused.

Kellan glanced at Jonah in surprise. He suspected Jonah was right and was impressed that he'd come to that conclusion as well. "With a two-front war and all the time and money they have invested in you, they're probably more than willing to look the other way as long as you're not obvious."

"They're already gearing up to implement the repeal," said Jonah. "It's going to happen, it's just a matter of when."

Kellan was surprised by Jonah's confidence and candor. Scuttlebutt on the Hill was that DADT was terminal. That belief had made its way to the troop level, too. That made Kellan happy on both a professional and a personal level.

"So, are you catching a ride with me, tomorrow?" he asked.

"If you don't mind." Jonah said quietly, looking at Kellan sidelong.

Kellan held out his hand which Jonah immediately clasped in his own. "I would very much enjoy it."

Chapter 2

It was a long fucking drive from Santa Barbara to the campus of UCLA. Despite the ample leg room and comfortable car, Kellan was stiff as he stepped out of the back seat and stretched. He looked over the roof of the limo and realized it had to be worse for Jonah, since he was several inches taller than Kellan.

Jonah walked in a circle, squaring away his uniform, his dress shoes clicking sharply on the pavement. He wore his olive uniform trousers and short sleeved khaki shirt, resplendent with his service and combat ribbons and medals. He was so fucking handsome, and so unaware of that fact, it made Kellan's heart swell.

"You must be Gunnery Sergeant Carver," said a voice behind Kellan. "Mr. Reynolds?"

Kellan turned and shook hands with an older, distinguished looked man dressed in a suit.

"I'm Kellan Reynolds," he replied. "And yes, this is Gunnery Sergeant Jonah Carver."

"I'm Doctor Stephen Holland," the man greeted. "It's an honor to have the two of you at the symposium."

This was not Kellan's and Jonah's first joint speaking engagement, and it didn't appear as though it would be their last. The ramifications of the events of that week in Iraq were still being felt around the country. His and Jonah's Senate testimony had riveted the nation, much to Jonah's chagrin.

"It's a pleasure to be here," Kellan replied.

"It's an honor, Doctor," Jonah said, shaking the professor's hand with all the typical confidence of a Marine.

Inside the large lecture hall, Doctor Holland showed them to a row of seats reserved for the various speakers and their guests. He took the podium, asked for the house lights to be dimmed, and welcomed the attendees to the UCLA Symposium on Military Infrastructure and

Corruption. In addition to Holland's Doctoral candidates, the attendees included both military and civilians who worked in the defense industry. There were many uniforms mixed in with the civvies.

The spotlight over the podium dimmed and a video presentation began on the oversized screen on the wall. It was a series of clips from the Senate hearings into the scandal that had all come to head in Diyala Province, Iraq. The clips included sound bites of both Kellan's and Jonah's prepared statements, as well as their answers to questions asked by the committee members.

"Our first speaker is a graduate of Princeton University," Holland said when the podium spotlight came up again. "He joined the Marine Corps upon his graduation, successfully completing Officer Candidate School and accepting his commission as a Second Lieutenant. After serving in both Iraq and Afghanistan and obtaining the rank of captain, he was honorably discharged, at which time he obtained a double Master's degree from Harvard University, in Business and Political Science. When his mentor, Phil Bowen, left the consulting firm he'd founded, to become a Deputy Secretary of Defense, our guest was appointed CEO of Keystone Consulting. He's agreed to speak to us today about the corruption he helped to uncover that led to the indictment of the three largest private security contractors. Please welcome, Mr. Kellan Reynolds."

Kellan was well practiced in providing the highlights of the events that had led to him accompanying an FBI team to Diyala Province in Iraq to investigate the murders of U.S. citizens, including many military personnel. He used his PowerPoint presentation to illustrate the trail of bribery and collusion that had led to more murders and eventually, to prosecutions. Afterward, he took questions from the audience.

The questions he was asked tended to be the same each time he spoke, and centered on information that wasn't released to the press or had been redacted from the official documents released to the public.

The questions gradually became more general, reflecting Kellan's acknowledged expertise in national security and the military's role in it.

A young man in civilian attire, but sporting an obviously military haircut, stood up. "Mr. Reynolds, to what do you attribute the significant reduction in the number of medals that have been awarded to U.S. service members in the last eight years, in contrast to the numbers awarded during previous wars?"

Kellan frowned. That was not a question he'd ever been asked before. He was sure the young man had his own agenda, but that didn't mean he didn't have a valid point to make. "I wasn't aware there was a significant reduction in the number of medals being awarded. What's your source?"

"The U.S. Department of Defense," the young man replied. "It's a matter of public record."

Kellan knew that to be true. "I admit, I've never been asked this question before so I don't have the information I need to formulate an answer," he admitted. "You've peaked my interest though, and I'm going to look into it if for no other reason than to assuage my own curiosity."

"As a veteran of both Iraq and Afghanistan, doesn't the possibility that this might be true bother you?" the man pressed.

Kellan carefully considered the question and his answer. "Not necessarily. The nature of modern warfare has changed dramatically. There is much less face-to-face combat and much more automation."

"What if that same technology is being used to change the standards used to award the medals?" the man asked.

"I need more information before I can address that." Kellan stood his ground. He was curious, though. He just couldn't afford to get bogged down in this discussion right now.

Kellan moved the discussion forward, taking other questions. He forgot about the young man until it was Jonah's turn to speak.

They were often asked to speak at the same events since their experiences were two sides of the same coin. Kellan was a policy expert with access to the President and the Departments of Defense and State. Jonah saw and felt the practical impact of events and decisions at the troop level. It was Kellan's involvement in an investigation that had gotten him abducted, but it was Jonah who had rescued him.

"Gunnery Sergeant Carver, are you at all bothered by the significant reduction in the number of medals that have been awarded to U.S. service members in the last eight years, in contrast to the numbers awarded during previous wars?"

Kellan recognized the voice of the young man who had asked him a similar question earlier. He turned in his seat to look at the man as he faced down Jonah across the lecture hall.

"That question puts me in an awkward position and makes it impossible for me to answer," Jonah said, his features sharp and his gaze direct. "As a recipient of the Navy Cross for my actions surrounding Mr. Reynold's abduction, I run the risk of calling into question the validity of my own award, as well as many other deserving sailors and Marines. Do I believe more service personal should receive medals? Absolutely. Do I question the process by which the awards are determined? That's above my paygrade, and that's the last I'm going to comment on the subject."

Kellan's eyebrows rose at both Jonah's eloquence, and at the blatantly confrontational way he dealt with the young man. As always, Kellan was impressed and more than a little aroused.

That evening, Kellan collapsed into the back seat of the limousine. Jonah did the same, tossing his barracks cover onto the leather seat across from them. Kellan opened a small bottle of diet soda. "Have we ever had limo sex?" he asked.

"No," Jonah answered tiredly, "and we're not going to now."

Kellan looked over at him in surprise. Jonah was usually up for anything. "We're not?"

Gesturing a hand the length of his own body, Jonah replied, "Uniform."

"How could I have forgotten?" Kellan asked seriously. He'd once been subject to the same grooming standard. He knew Jonah took the rules of wearing a Marine Corps uniform seriously. It was an honor Jonah didn't fuck with.

"We'll have to rent our own limo soon so I can wear civvies," Jonah said with a grin. "Then you can have your limo sex."

"I'll hold you to that," Kellan chuckled. He remembered a time just a few years prior when he'd said those words to Jonah under much more serious circumstances.

"Can you at least wait until we get back to the hotel?" Jonah asked.

Kellan sighed dramatically. "If I must."

There was nothing that said he couldn't make the ride back with his head on Jonah's shoulder, so he did.

Chapter 3

Kellan was stretched out in an oversized chair, his legs propped on the matching ottoman. His laptop sat open on top of his thighs as he read through a folder of hard copy reports.

Jonah slid down the arm of the chair until he was sitting next to Kellan, pressed up against the length of his side.

"Something really doesn't seem right here," Kellan said, not looking away from the papers in his hand.

"Is that the information on the medals awarded to OIF and OEF veterans?" Jonah asked, squinting to read.

Kellan sighed heavily and gave a slow shake of his head. "Yeah. Just looking at Medals of Honor and nothing else, and making a comparison to the Vietnam war, at least 270 more medals should have been awarded by now, given the length of the two current conflicts."

Jonah tensed beside him. "Is it possibly because the number of troops that have actually deployed is lower?" he finally asked. "Technology has come a long way, we're doing a lot more with less personnel."

Kellan had already considered that. "If you calculate the MOH's awarded in both world wars, Korea, and Vietnam, it comes out to be between twenty-three and twenty-nine medals for every one million troops."

"I take it's lower for Iraq and Afghanistan?" Jonah asked dubiously.

"It's one," Kellan replied incredulously. "It's one Medal of Honor awarded for everyone million troops deployed to Iraq and Afghanistan in almost nine years of war."

They sat in tense silence for several long moments. "Okay," Jonah finally said, "you said yourself that we're utilizing more *standoff* weapons, like drones and attack aircraft. Maybe there are fewer opportunities for individual valor?"

"That's what this is." Kellan indicated the thick folder of hard copy reports. "I pulled a large number of random citations for the MOH from all the twentieth-century wars and conflicts, as well as the citations for Iraq and Afghanistan Distinguished Service Crosses, Navy Crosses, Air Force Crosses and even the Silver Star. These lesser citations read like Medal of Honor citations awarded in World War Two or Vietnam."

"So, what's your preliminary theory?" asked Jonah.

Kellan thumbed through the papers, searching for a specific Silver Star citation. "That the military command structure, made up of old, white men who served in Korea and Vietnam, are holding an all-volunteer military that is as racially diverse as it's ever been, that's moving more women than ever to the forward lines, and is about to allow homosexuals to serve openly, to a nearly impossible to achieve standard."

Jonah groaned as if he was in pain. "Is this the same way you ended up in Iraq with me trying to keep you from taking a beating?"

Kellan chuckled. "No. Back then I was actually trying to prove a point and impress someone. Now I'm just feeding my own curiosity. They based the denial of Miguel Restrepo the MOH on criteria never used before."

"Would you be this curious if Restrepo had been a soldier instead of a Marine?" Jonah searched his face intently.

"I don't know," Kellan replied honestly. "But I'm distinctly uncomfortable with how they've called into question the word and the honor of an entire platoon of Marines."

Jonah nodded his understanding. "Keep me posted." He gathered up the folder of papers, closed Kellan's laptop, and set everything on the floor beside the chair. "Now, you can obsesses about this when I'm back in California." His voice was pitched low and full of promise. "I'm only here for another week, so you should be obsessing about me."

Kellan settled back in the chair, his heart kicking up in pace. He enjoyed the feel of Jonah's heat beside him. "I always obsesses about you. Any news on your billet?" Jonah had been allowed to attend the 1st Sergeant Course once his selection to 1st Sergeant was confirmed, but before he was technically promoted. They were waiting to hear where he'd be assigned once his promotion was implemented.

"Yeah, I heard days ago and I forgot to tell you." Jonah's sarcasm was palpable.

"Okay, stupid question," Kellan said, raising his hands in supplication. "You know why I'm impatient."

"Yeah, I know," Jonah whispered, lowering his head for a gentle kiss.

Kellan slid his hands beneath Jonah's shirt, feeling warm, smooth skin beneath his palms. Jonah moaned softly, arching into Kellan's hands. Kellan rubbed his tongue against Jonah's before it retreated. He chased Jonah's mouth, opening immediately to him when Jonah changed the angle of the kiss. Jonah pulled back again, tilted his head and nipped at Kellan's lower lip. Kellan lay back and let Jonah have his way. He watched Jonah's wet, reddened lips each time he pulled back and closed his eyes in pleasure each time Jonah leaned in for a kiss.

"Let's get this out of the way," Jonah murmured, tugging Kellan's shirt awkwardly over his head.

Kellan ran his hands over Jonah's back. He wanted to feel that warm skin pressed against his own. "You, too," he said between heated kisses, pulling at the hem of Jonah's shirt until he dragged it over his head.

He pulled Jonah to him, taking Jonah's weight as he draped himself over Kellan's body. Kellan moaned at the wet rub of their tongues against each other as Jonah kept his lips just out of reach. It was the kind of dirty kiss Jonah had gotten Kellan hooked on.

Jonah slid down Kellan's body and straddled his legs. Kellan watched him, cheeks flushed, lips red and swollen as he breathed heavily through them. Jonah's long fingered hands, as gentle as they were deadly, tugged at the waist of Kellan's track pants. Kellan helped him, pushing the fabric downward and freeing his still-growing erection. He watched his own cock settle against his belly and give a single, impatient twitch.

Kellan gripped the base, holding his dick upright as encouragement for Jonah to do what they both wanted him to. Whenever Jonah did this for him, Kellan couldn't help remembering their first time together. He'd wanted Jonah badly from the first moment they'd met. As Jonah's platoon commander, Kellan hadn't dared act on his desires. The night he'd told Jonah he was leaving the Marines, he'd been hoping the attraction was mutual and that he could finally know what it was like to be with Jonah.

That first night in the bedroom of Kellan's small, rented house, when Jonah had knelt before him and sucked him down was seared into Kellan's memory. He'd been a fool to let distance and DADT come between. For five lonely years he'd mistaken Jonah's reserve for indifference.

Jonah's fingers twined with his own at the base of his cock. Kellan sucked a deep, audible breath in through his nose at the sight and feel of Jonah's mouth sliding down around his length.

"Fuck that feels good," he said on an exhale. Kellan squeezed himself a little harder, battling for control. The wet heat of Jonah's mouth was intense, all consuming. Kellan watched his blond head move rhythmically up and down as Jonah sucked him. The flat press of Jonah's tongue against the underside of his cock made Kellan's hips flex upward, trying to get just a little deeper.

Jonah's lips were stretched wide around his width and Kellan reached out with his free hand to trace the corner of his mouth. He felt the head of his own erection glide against the inside of Jonah's mouth. Kellan pressed the pad of his thumb to a spot where Jonah's lips met his cock.

Kellan gasped when Jonah's blue eyes flicked up to meet his. Jonah looked at him questioningly but didn't break his rhythm.

"So, fucking hot to watch you sucking me," Kellan murmured, caressing Jonah's wet lips. "Feels so good."

Jonah's fingers stayed twined with Kellan's where they both gripped the base of Kellan's cock. Kellan cupped Jonah's cheek, skimming his thumb over the sharp bone and feeling Jonah's mouth working him relentlessly. Jonah slid his free hand up Kellan's hip and brought it to rest against his stomach, more affectionate than restraining.

Kellan tightened his grip on the base of his erection as a tingle swept through his balls and spiraled into his belly. Jonah watched him intently, eyes narrowed as he kept up his pace and tightened his suction. Each time he pulled back to the head of Kellan's cock, Jonah left the shaft glistening wetly with his spit. The sight was like a punch to Kellan's gut and his orgasm built up more quickly, his ball sac tightening.

"Fuck," Kellan breathed. "I'm gonna come, you're gonna make me come," he whispered hastily, fingers tightening on his cock and on Jonah's cheek.

Jonah pulled off all the way, moving slowly and rising to his knees. He smiled wickedly down at Kellan, mouth red and swollen, eyes luminous. "I love the sounds you make when I suck your dick," he said. "I love to make you feel good."

Kellan made a surprised noise when Jonah abruptly grasped his hips and tugged him down lower in the chair. Before Kellan could recover, Jonah was pulling his track pants over his hips and off his legs. Kellan's heart beat faster in anticipation. He'd lost track of how many times they'd done this in the last week, but he couldn't get enough. Neither had any idea when they would have the chance again.

He watched Jonah open the fly of his own shorts. Kellan didn't resist when Jonah gripped him by the knees and lifted. He was spread open for Jonah to admire and touch as he wanted.

Jonah frowned, expression darkening. He tilted his head at a different angle and worry marred his handsome features.

Kellan's stomach lurched. "What?" he asked, mind racing over what it was that could so rapidly cool Jonah's ardor.

"I've hurt you," Jonah said quietly. With one hand, he gently caressed Kellan's asshole, using just the tips of his fingers. "You're red and swollen. I didn't know. Why didn't you say something?"

Kellan shook his head in confusion. Jonah had pounded into him over and over in the last week and he'd enjoyed every single second. He'd grown slightly tender in the last day, but certainly not enough to prevent them from enjoying each other again, or to warrant the obvious distress on Jonah's face.

"There's nothing to say," Kellan said with an embarrassed chuckle. "I've been well fucked but I'm not in pain."

Jonah continued to caress Kellan's hole. Kellan flexed his hips, his muscles clenching in excitement and anticipation. He wanted Jonah to slip his fingers inside, to push into Kellan's ass and fill him up again.

"We'll do something else, this time," Jonah said, sitting back on his heels and lowering Kellan's legs. "Give you a chance to rest and heal."

Kellan's eyes dropped to the prominent bulge in the front of Jonah's shorts. There were lots of other things they could do and Jonah was pretty damn good at all of them, but Kellan only wanted one thing.

"I don't need to rest and there's nothing to heal," he assured Jonah. "We can't go dry again, so just get the lube and use plenty of it."

"Kel, I don't need..."

"But I want to," Kellan interrupted Jonah's protest. "Get the lube, get naked and fuck me, for Chrissake."

"Jesus," Jonah whispered, gripping himself through the front of his shorts, his face flushing deeper red.

He slid off the ottoman and disappeared, returning quickly with their partially used bottle of lubricant. Jonah hastily shed his shorts before once again kneeling between Kellan's legs. Kellan admired Jonah's erection as it stood proudly from the dark blond nest of curls. He loved the feel of Jonah's cock when it slid past his rim and deep into his ass.

Kellan lifted and spread his legs, opening himself to Jonah. He smiled encouragingly.

Jonah doused his fingers generously with lube. "Are you sure you're okay?"

Kellan stroked his erection languidly and met Jonah's gaze. "I'm a big boy, I *can* take care of myself."

Jonah looked as though Kellan's response had caught him off guard. He snorted a laugh. "That's kind of hard to miss."

Kellan hissed at the cold when Jonah's fingers pressed to his tender hole. Jonah frowned in concern. Kellan bit down on his lower lip to keep from laughing at Jonah's obvious distress. His laugh turned to a moan when one of Jonah's fingers breached him. The smooth glide of Jonah's finger inside of him eased the sting of his opening. Kellan was still slick from Jonah's loving from that morning as well as the evening before. They only needed to be careful of his tender rim.

Jonah withdrew his finger and added more lubricant. Kellan sighed in pleasure when Jonah circled his opening with two gel-covered fingers. Now, the cool slick was soothing. The sensitive bundles of nerves made the ring of muscle clench. Kellan breathed deeply and reminded himself to relax.

A dollop of lube slide down the crease of Kellan's ass and Jonah's fingers caught it and smeared it against his hole.

"You're a fucking tease, Jonah," Kellan said on a laugh, squirming against the pressure of Jonah's fingers pushing into him again.

"I'm afraid to hurt you again," Jonah said, voice tight.

"You haven't hurt me, yet," Kellan replied quickly.

He watched Jonah smooth lube over his reddened erection, making it shiny with slick. Jonah aligned the head of his cock with Kellan's hole. Kellan gripped Jonah's ribcage as he leaned forward and loomed over. Jonah propped himself on the arm and the back of the chair and Kellan wrapped his legs around Jonah's hips.

"Tell me if I hurt you," Jonah said in a strained voice. "I'll stop if you need me to." He stared into Kellan's eyes as he started to move.

Kellan arched and cried out when Jonah flexed his hips and pushed past the swollen, sensitive flesh of his opening. Jonah's eyes widened and he stopped moving.

"Oh god, don't stop," Kellan gasped, tugging Jonah closer with his hands and his legs.

Jonah pressed forward, Kellan's hole stinging and burning. His inner muscles relaxed easily, the comfortable familiarity of Jonah's cock sending pleasure shooting up his spine. Jonah's thighs met Kellan's ass cheeks and the base of his cock stretched Kellan's hole, bringing back the sting and the burn. Kellan gasped.

Jonah froze but he never looked away from Kellan's eyes. "Okay?" he gasped.

"Fuck yeah," Kellan groaned, sliding his hands down Jonah's back to grip his ass and encourage him to move.

Slowly at first, Jonah moved in and out of Kellan's body. Kellan smiled up at him, watching Jonah's flush deepen and is eyes brighten. Their harsh breathing was loud in the quiet room, punctuated by the sound of skin on skin. Each inward flex of Jonah's hips filled Kellan's ass. Every few thrusts, Jonah circled his hips and the head of his cock subtly brushed against Kellan's sweet spot. He moaned softly each time, telling Jonah he was getting it just right.

"Fuck," Jonah said in what sounded like a quiet sob. The weight of his body settled over Kellan, the heat of his skin warming Kellan where they touched. "You feel so good. I'm so fucking close already."

Kellan wrapped his arms around Jonah's chest, amazed at how quickly Jonah's climax had come on. They'd fucked so often during the last week, it was surprising either of them had anything left.

Jonah's breath was hot against Kellan's skin where he'd buried his face against Kellan's neck. Kellan cried out when Jonah picked up his rhythm and changed the angle of his thrusts. Each inward stroke nailed Kellan's prostate.

"Jesus Christ," Kellan shouted, a violent shudder rolling through him. He couldn't catch his breath. He clutched at Jonah's back and clung to him.

"Come on, Kel. Come for me. Wanna feel you come." Jonah was murmuring against Kellan's throat.

He could hardly hear Jonah's words, Kellan's own breathing and cries nearly drowned him out. Kellan reached between their bodies and wrapped his hand around his own aching, leaking cock. With Jonah slamming against his gland relentlessly, Kellan was instantly on the verge of coming. He stroked himself in time with Jonah's hips, his inner muscles clenching at Jonah and his balls tightening and lifting.

"How the fuck do you do that?" Jonah asked in a strangled voice just before he slammed into Kellan's body and froze.

Kellan's muscles locked up and he tightened around Jonah's cock, buried deep inside of him. Even as the first hot splash of come landed between their bodies, Kellan felt Jonah pulse deep inside of him. Liquid heat flooded him yet again, even as it covered the skin of their chests and bellies.

Jonah collapsed on top of him. Kellan knew their positions in the chair would be uncomfortable in a few minutes, but he didn't care. He liked the feel of Jonah against him and inside of him. He dreaded the flare of pain he knew was coming when Jonah pulled out. Kellan really was going to have to give his hole a rest now. It was okay, he could think of a lot of things he could do to Jonah in the meantime.

He just needed some rest first.

Chapter 4

Kellan still wasn't used to meeting with Senators without first being heavily screened by staffers. That had all changed with his involvement in the prosecution of the private contractors who had supplied enemy forces in Iraq with munitions in order to perpetuate the conflict. He'd proven himself as an expert in national security and brought himself to the attention of some important people in government with his Senate testimony.

Senator Gilchrist's Chief of Staff showed Kellan into the meeting room where an assistant offered him coffee or water. Kellan accepted a bottle of water. He shook hands with Senators Gilchrist, Lopes and Billings before taking the seat they offered.

Gilchrist was a veteran of the Korean conflict. He still carried himself like a military man and sported a distinguished looking head of silver hair. "That was an interesting report Keystone Consulting published this week," the Senator said. "Well researched, succinctly stated, and extremely compelling."

"Thank you, Senator," Kellan replied, waiting for the other shoe to drop.

"Why did you publish this information in this manner?" asked Senator Billings. She was a handsome woman, serving her fifth term in the Senate. "Why not address your concerns to the Senate Armed Services Committee, the Joint Chiefs, or the Department of Defense?"

"Please don't be cagey, Senator Billings, it insults us both," said Kellan. "You know I know that you sat on the committee that held hearings in 2008 to address the egregious lack of medals awarded for our two current conflicts. The military establishment is well aware of this issue. Given that your hearings went nowhere in oh-eight, that leads me to believe that they aren't concerned. Certainly not enough to address the issue."

Billings smiled indulgently. "They warned me not to underestimate you, Mr. Reynolds," she said. "So, you're attempting to generate public sentiment for your cause."

"It's not my cause, Senator," replied Kellan. "It's a set of facts taken within a certain context. It does seem to indicate an imbalance at best, an injustice at worst."

"If we decided to make this a cause," Senator Lopes interjected smoothly, "would you be willing to work with us in an investigative and advisory capacity?" Lopes was a youthful man of obvious Hispanic heritage. He was already establishing a reputation for reason and moderation, while still fighting diligently for the rights of all ethnic groups.

"As much as the Marine captain in me would like to pick a side in this issue," Kellan answered carefully, "my role as CEO of Keystone Consulting demands impartiality."

"I believe that's what we're asking, Mr. Reynolds," Gilchrist said. "Are you willing and able to step outside of your role as CEO of your consulting firm with regard to this issue?"

"You mean act as a private consultant?" Kellan asked incredulously.

"More as a public consultant," replied Gilchrist. "On the payroll of the United States Senate, taking guidance from and providing guidance to, ourselves and the President."

"The President?" Kellan was wary now. Access was coveted and often dangled as incentive.

Gilchrist splayed his hands, palms up. "He's the Commander in Chief of the Armed Forces and has a vested interest in their welfare and morale."

Kellan's mind raced. He had come here prepared to defend his position or to provide additional information. He hadn't anticipated a job offer. He pressed his fingertips to his lips thoughtfully.

"We don't expect your answer right now," Senator Billings said, interrupting Kellan's thoughts. "You need time to consider it, discuss it with family and staff."

"Speaking of staff," said Kellan abruptly, "it would be unethical to utilize Keystone staff for any of this work."

"We don't expect you to work alone, Mr. Reynolds." Gilchrist seemed surprised. "The offer includes a full staff that you would assemble. You'll need at least an assistant and a few investigators."

"Most likely a military liaison, as well," remarked Lopes.

"Jonah Carver is a First Sergeant now, isn't he?" Billings asked. "His transfer to MCCMOS at Quantico could be delayed for the duration of this project."

Kellan struggled to suppress his smile. He wasn't worried that these Senators seemed to know something; they were all pushing for the repeal of DADT.

"If I can have a week to see if I'm able to line up staff," Kellan proposed. "Discuss this with my staff at Keystone and a few of my own personal advisors."

"Absolutely, Mr. Reynolds," Gilchrist said with gracious enthusiasm. "And please, advise us of any concerns or requests you have. There is much we can do to accommodate you in order to get you on board."

Kellan stood and shook their hands once again. "Thank you, Senators. I'll be in touch."

• • • •

"I WAS JOKING WHEN I told you it was okay to obsess about this once I was back in California," Jonah said, completely devoid of humor.

"I didn't obsess," Kellan countered. "I followed up on information that is a matter of public record. This type of thing is actually my *job*."

"Yes, and obviously you're doing it quite well. No surprise there. So, initial thoughts?"

"I think this is a real problem and I'd like to see something done about it," Kellan replied, giving his personal, emotional answer. "The challenge and opportunity excite me, but I have no desire to damage or sacrifice my current situation."

"In other words; you're interested, but under the right conditions."

"That's it exactly." Kellan sighed, relieved by the ease with which Jonah understood and accepted.

"Fall back on your training, sir. Use S-M-E-A-C to clarify the complex."

Kellan took a deep breath and let it out slowly, his mind racing and already extracting and aligning the relevant information. SMEAC was the mnemonic for the five paragraph written order, utilized by officers to clearly issue complex orders; situation, mission, execution, administration & logistics, and command & signal.

"The situation is that there is a questionable policy or policy implementation that needs investigation or possible intervention," Kellan said. "The mission is to determine the full extent of the problem, causes, parties responsible, and to provide potential solutions."

"That was the easy part," Jonah said, sounding as though he was shuffling paperwork as they talked. *"Now you have to determine just what your course of action would be, what you'd need, and if you think you can actually accomplish anything."*

Kellan consulted the legal pad in front of him. He'd already done this work. What Jonah was doing now was giving Kellan the opportunity to say it all out loud, to face his fears and worries. In doing so, he'd establish whether or not this was a fool's errand.

"Execution is going to involve submitting requests for documents under the Freedom of Information Act. Obtaining other documents through Senate requests and demands. Interviews will need to be conducted, reports written and filed. Ruffled feathers will have to be smoothed, military policy and ROE established and analyzed." Kellan paused. "That can all be done by staff. In the end, I'll have to be the one to put the disparate parts together, formulate logical conclusions, write summaries and reports and report the findings to the Senate, the President, and other government officials of varying levels of hostility."

"That leads you to administration and logistics," Jonah said.

"If I could have my dream team, I'd bring Maddy and Nick with me from Keystone to handle filings, interviews, document and report, review and compilation, and also analysis." Kellan checked their names off of the list on his legal pad. "I'd like to have a J.A.G. lawyer or someone from J.A.S. to both advise and interpret U.S., military and international law."

"How about a paralegal or a legal secretary, then?" Jonah asked.

"Definitely. That might be pushing things, though," replied Kellan. "I've already been told I can have you as my military liaison to smooth the way with the uniforms. My former rank might not get me as far as I'd like to think."

Jonah's chuckle warmed Kellan's chest and he smiled in response, even though Jonah couldn't see. *"You assume I'd be willing to assist you in your bureaucratic tail-chasing, sir."*

"It would provide us with a legitimate reason for why we were constantly in one another's company," Kellan teased.

"Point, sir," Jonah conceded. *"Anyone else?"*

"A strong and self-motivated civilian executive assistant to answer phones, email, handle paperwork and just generally keep me organized and on time," stated Kellan.

"A nearly impossible task," Jonah said dryly. *"This person already has my pity. Who else do you think you need?"*

"I'd like to have one or two additional investigators who *don't* have ties to Keystone," Kellan told him. "Possibly an MP, NCIS or FBI agent."

"You already know a couple of Feebs with expertise in national security as well as the military conditions in Iraq," Jonah said pointedly.

"Yes, I do, don't I?" Kellan acknowledged. "We would need to work out of either D.C. or So Cal, quite possibly both. And we would all need access to basic office equipment and softwares."

"That touches on command & signal," observed Jonah.

"Again, in a perfect world, I'd like to rent offices in both D.C. and Oceanside and have access to the obvious equipment," Kellan stated. "Everyone would report directly to me until such time as I delegated projects or tasks."

"Please don't make me your second in command," Jonah complained.

Kellan laughed. "As a first shirt, you'd function as my exec. If I could get an attorney, I'd designate that person as next in the chain of command, otherwise one of the investigative agents."

Jonah sighed heavily, the sound carrying easily over the connection. *"You and I both agree that the under awarding of Medals of Honor is a serious issue that needs addressing and changing. At the very least, someone needs to have the balls to stand up and admit why the awards are intentionally blocked."*

"Agreed."

"What are the benefits to our lives and our careers if we do this?" asked Jonah. *"And what damage could it do, if any?"*

Kellan took a deep breath. They'd reached the heart of his conflict. This was what he needed to talk out with someone. This was what he desperately needed Jonah's input on. If Kellan was alone, he'd have already accepted the job and jumped in with both feet. *He* was now a *we* and he needed Jonah's agreement and moral support, even if he couldn't give his professional help.

Before Kellan could answer, Jonah spoke again, *"Just tell me this, Kel; is your gut telling you we need to do this?"*

"Yes." Kellan didn't hesitate. "Yes, it is."

"Then I guess someone is going to have to delay my transfer to MC-CMOS. I guess I can move to the barracks at eighth and aye, unless you know of someone with a room to rent?"

Kellan's heart sank when he realized Jonah had no desire to move in with him when he transferred to Virginia. He swallowed hard, determined to keep his voice steady and not give any hint as to how disappointed he was.

Jonah made a quiet sound that sounded almost like a muffled laugh. Kellan's mouth dropped open when he realized he'd been had. He couldn't believe he'd fallen for it, however briefly.

"No, you go ahead and move into a fucking Marine Corps barracks." Kellan coated each word heavily in sarcasm. "You stretch out that six-foot-three-inch body on one of those cots they call beds. I'll be here, in my big, comfortable house with my soft, king sized bed. Have I mentioned I sleep naked?"

"Okay, okay," Jonah burst out laughing. *"I deserved that."* There was a long pause. Kellan could feel the mood grow serious, even over the cell phone connection. *"Are you sure you have room for me and my stuff, Kel?"*

"Jonah," Kellan answered softly, "I always have room for you. Always."

Chapter 5

Kellan sipped at his cup of coffee, listening with half an ear to the conversation around the small conference table. His staff of investigators, working on behalf of the Senate committee looking into the questionable policies on the awarding of the Medal of Honor, was gathering to discuss the controversial denial of a Medal to a Marine. Captain Mirai Hirata, the lawyer with the Marine Corps' Judge Advocate Services and NCIS Special Agent Chris Hoffman had flown in from Camp Pendleton the night before and were expected to arrive from their hotel any moment.

Beside him, Jonah warmed his own coffee from the carafe in the center of the table. He had to give his assistant credit, she was good at setting up for meetings. Her work in other areas was mediocre, but Kellan wasn't in a position to complain. She'd been provided by the FBI because they had needed someone quickly, who had the requisite security clearances. If he were honest, she wasn't a bad assistant, she just wasn't as good as his assistant at Keystone.

"They took a cab so they can't be lost," Nick said, looking at his watch with a frown.

"It's more likely jet lag and the change in time zones," Jonah remarked.

Kellan tugged his sleeve up to look at his watch. It was only 0805, he wasn't concerned. It was probably traffic. Nick was notoriously impatient. Kellan smiled as Maddy yawned noisily. She proclaimed herself to not be a morning person, yet still managed to always be the first one into the office each day.

FBI Special Agent Marco Giammona picked up his cell phone when it vibrated. "Traffic," he announced, "Chris says they're getting out of the cab downstairs now."

Just as he'd suspected. "Thanks, Marco." Kellan had been pleased when Marco had agreed to come work for him. He'd been impressed with the Agent's work and his testimony in the wake of the events in Diyala.

A ruckus in the outer offices announced the arrival of Hirata and Hoffman. They were greeted warmly by the rest of the staff. For all they had done the majority of their work on the west coast, they had proven to be very, very good at their jobs. It was their work that had everyone gathered today to discuss what appeared to be a very ugly problem.

"All rights, gents," Kellan called the meeting to order. "And lady," he said, smiling at Maddy, "let's get started. Chris? Mirai? Who wants to start?"

"I will," Chris replied, handing out stapled packets of paper. "The Defense Secretary's recent rejection of the petition to upgrade the Navy Cross to the Medal of Honor for Sergeant Miguel Restrepo appears to be problematic for two reasons. It's yet another in a long line of denials that would clearly have been worthy of the MOH in previous conflicts. However, it's the first time a scientific panel has been convened to establish and consider forensic evidence, and that all eyewitness testimony of Marines present during the incident has been disregarded completely."

"I can already tell that those two issues are linked," Kellan said, skimming through the document and seeing a thorough investigation had been conducted. "Technology has changed everything about warfare. It's reasonable to expect it to be utilized to determine the worthiness of a medal citation, and that it would affect the outcome of many of those decisions."

"That would be both reasonable and expected," said Captain Hirata. "One would then expect that the criteria for all medals would be revised to accommodate the changes in technology, but they have not. The process for determination remains unchanged, yet we're all aware that the application of those criteria has altered for some inexplicable reason."

"In Restrepo's case, it appears as though a new standard was implemented with the intention of denying him the MOH?" Jonah asked.

"In light of the fact that an independent medical panel reviewed the same information and reached a completely different conclusion, that seems likely," answered Hoffman.

"My next question would be whether technology has changed the nature of our combat to the extent that fewer opportunities for individual valor are available," mused Kellan. "But we've already established that both battles of Fallujah, the regular clearing of houses at the platoon level, and the ongoing campaign to win hearts and minds negates that argument completely."

"That's correct," Hoffman confirmed.

"Has a larger pattern emerged?" Kellan asked, sitting back in his chair and spinning his ink stick between his fingers to ease his agitation.

"Not one that I can prove in a court of law," Hirata answered.

"So, what do you know that you can't prove?" Jonah asked.

Agent Giammona cleared his throat and sat forward in his chair, passing out another thick packet of papers. "That the military establishment is systematically under-awarding medals to the members of the first all-volunteer military in U.S. history," he summarized. "The underlying belief is that because they are all volunteers and are not conscripted, that they understand and accept what they're getting into and that makes their actions less heroic and more," he paused, as if considering his words, "the expected standard."

Kellan sat in stunned silence and could feel Jonah's growing tension radiating off of him.

"That may be the polite face the Pentagon is putting on the situation, though," Maddy said into the tense silence. "This all-volunteer military is made up of more people of color, more women, more homosexuals, and more foreign nationals than ever before."

"There *is* a publicly acknowledged history of racial discrimination in the awarding of the MOH," Hirata added.

"All nine of the recipients of the MOH from OIF and OEF are white men," Nick said, taking a set of photos from a folder and laying them out for Kellan to see.

"And that's another thing, Kellan," Maddy said, "nine medals total, awarded in two separate wars. One-hundred-ninety-three Medals of Honor have been awarded for peace-time incidents. How does that make sense?"

Kellan tossed his pen down on the table and rubbed both hands over his face in annoyance. "Well, shit," he said darkly, staring blindly at the table in front of him, mind racing over the implications and his possible options.

Suddenly, Jonah sat forward in his chair and pinned each staff member with a direct look. "Kellan needs to know two things so he can decide the most appropriate course, or courses of action moving forward: Captain Hirata currently couldn't prove our case in a court of law, but are all of you able to compile a case that he could prove? If the answer to that question is yes, do all of you have the desire and fortitude to see this through to its conclusion?"

Kellan looked into the determined faces of his staff. Nick and Maddy had little to lose. They were civilians and Kellan wasn't going to hold their involvement against them. Agent Giammona was with the FBI and could possibly incur the wrath of his superiors, but it wasn't likely. Agent Hoffman and Captain Hirata, however, could face fallout if the Navy or the Marine Corps took exception to anything they might uncover or do during the course of this investigation.

They had a little Senatorial protection, but it only extended so far and Kellan was only just building up his own political clout.

"When Kellan first asked me to sign on for this, I knew it could get sticky," Maddy was the first to reply. "I signed on to see this through to the end, whatever Kellan decides the end is."

As she spoke, Nick sat beside her, mutely nodding his agreement. Kellan nodded his appreciation to them, touched by their dedication and loyalty.

"My participation is official, so I'm here unless or until the Bureau yanks me out," Marco said, shaking his head. There was obviously more he wanted to say. "A lot of the time, the work I do doesn't make much difference in the larger scheme of things. The supply of criminals is endless, and the ones I do catch don't always get their full measure of justice. This matters, though. This might not lead to anything technically criminal, but it's important to hold people accountable for good old fashioned right and wrong."

There were nods of agreement all around the table.

"Thank you, Marco." The simple didn't begin to express the depth of Kellan's appreciation.

"Mirai and I were discussing this on the flight out," said Chris. "We're going to end up fighting this battle on two fronts; the systematic denial of medals and the individual case of the obviously deserving Miguel Restrepo. But someone has to fight it, it's only right. So, the two of us are in until they lock us up for insubordination."

Hirata laughed quietly. "I'm a lawyer, I can probably figure out how to get the charges dropped."

The room erupted into laughter and Kellan joined in gratefully. It appeared his fears about this situation were proving true and it saddened him, even as it fired his anger and motivated him to action.

"Okay," Jonah addressed the group. "Kellan and I will discuss it, formulate our strategy and then we'll work out the details with all of you." He dismissed the group with a nod, even Captain Hirata responding to the natural authority.

When the door closed and they were alone, Jonah turned in his chair to face Kellan. "So, Captain, ready to go to war?"

Chapter 6

Kellan was escorted into the Pentagon office of the Secretary of Defense, Calvin Burnett. This appointment had been difficult to schedule. Senator Gilchrist had finally intervened, when the Secretary's staff kept trying to schedule Kellan a month out. As they had gathered preliminary information and he'd submitted reports to the Senators, Kellan had hoped they might uncover innocent or reasonable explanations for the scarce number of Medals of Honor awarded in the last decade. The silent wall of the Department of Defense had quickly killed that hope.

Jonah's expression was dark as he stood to watch Kellan enter Burnett's office. He was having a difficult time not taking their findings personally.

"Mr. Reynolds," Burnett greeted, shaking Kellan's hand. "Please have a seat."

The Secretary gestured toward a comfortable looking guest chair as he walked around behind his own impressive desk. Kellan sat, but Burnett did not. He remained standing and rifled through stacks of papers on his desk. It was rude, dismissive, and an obvious power play. Kellan was supposed to be intimidated. He wasn't. He was, however, angry and disappointed.

"What can I do for you today, Kellan?" Burnett sought to throw Kellan even further off balance with the familiarity.

"That's Mr. Reynolds, Secretary Burnett," Kellan replied, refusing to play the game. "I'm a retired Marine Corps captain, I have a double Masters degree from Harvard University, I'm the CEO of an influential consulting company, and a committee of Senators has asked me to conduct an investigation on their behalf. I'm not a junior staffer to be casually disregarded, so let's dispense with the games, shall we?"

Burnett looked up at him in surprise. "I wasn't aware we had engaged in any game playing," he said stiffly. "What is it we're meeting about today, *Mr. Reynolds?*"

Kellan allowed himself to savor a moment of victory. "You're fully aware of what I came here to discuss, Mr. Secretary," he said. "I made no secret about it when I requested this meeting. You've also had your staff investigate both my official mission, as well as the rumors that surround it."

Burnett laughed mirthlessly. "You're right, Mr. Reynolds. One doesn't become Secretary of Defense without knowing to have your staff learn everything possible about who you meet with. Unfortunately, my schedule is tight today, and I'm running behind. We're going to have to finish this talk on the way to my next meeting."

The Secretary started for the office door but Kellan didn't move. "That's much more subtle than having your assistant interrupt us in a few minutes with an emergency meeting you've been called into," he said dryly. "Mr. Secretary, I went through the proper channels and booked an hour of your time today. If you refuse me that full hour, I'll have no choice but to officially conclude that you knowingly denied Sergeant Restrepo the Medal of Honor for reasons of racism."

Burnett resumed his seat at his desk. He regarded Kellan for several moments before he sighed heavily. "The general consensus is that your separation from the Marine Corps was the Corps' loss," he said ruefully. "I think that assessment might be correct."

Kellan stored that away for future analysis.

"Mr. Secretary, I'm here to discuss your decision to uphold your predecessor's denial of Sergeant Miguel Restrepo the Medal of Honor." Kellan scrolled through the notes on his tablet app. "When we establish that this is part of a larger policy that systematically denies veterans of Iraq and Afghanistan the MOH, I'll be back to discuss that with you."

"I have no doubt of that, Mr. Reynolds," Burnett responded dryly.

Kellan continued as if he hadn't been interrupted. "The former Secretary of Defense, Harry Simpson, manufactured a method to discredit and disregard the eyewitness testimony of heroic Marines. You were handed a face-saving reason you could revise that decision and award Restrepo the medal, yet you chose not to take it."

"Is there a question in there somewhere, Mr. Reynolds?"

"There are several, Mr. Secretary," Kellan replied, undaunted. "Why is Sergeant Restrepo being held to a higher standard than every other MOH recipient? Why is the veracity of the testimony of United States Marines being questioned? Why did Simpson convene a medical panel for the first, and last time in the history of the awarding the MOH, without any official adjustment to standards and policies? When the findings of that panel were contradicted and disproved, why did you uphold them, Mr. Secretary?"

Kellan held the stylus poised above the screen of his tablet, prepared to make notes of Burnett's answers.

The Secretary exhaled harshly and sat back in his chair. He inhaled deeply before he spoke. "You may feel free to call me Cal, if I may call you Kellan," Burnett said placidly.

Kellan hoped he hid his surprise. He inclined his head, silently agreeing to the concession for which he had been asked.

"I'm going to have some coffee." Burnett sat forward and typed briefly on his laptop. "Would you like some coffee, Kellan?"

Kellan recognized the twenty-first century equivalent of the peace pipe. "I would appreciate that, Cal, thank you."

Minutes later, Burnett's assistant entered carrying a tray, laden with a carafe, two mugs, sweetener packets and a small pitcher of creamer. As Kellan prepared his coffee to his taste, the assistant said, "I'm making sure the Staff Sergeant is comfortable, Mr. Reynolds. He accepted a bottle of water when I offered."

"Thank you," Kellan said gratefully. He knew Jonah would be bored as hell, waiting for him, so at least he'd be comfortable.

When they were alone once again, Burnett regarded Kellan over the rim of his mug. "This conversation is off the record," he said abruptly. "I legitimately can't be of help to you, but I'm also not going to be a hindrance."

"I don't understand." Kellan was confused but the Secretary's words stirred hope, deep inside of him.

"I have no knowledge of a systematic denial of medals for racial or gender reasons," Burnett explained. "It's not something being encouraged, even subtly, from my office. When you build a case against anyone in the DOD who is guilty of that kind of discriminatory behavior, I won't stand in your way, or protect the guilty. But I can't help you with building that portion of your case."

Kellan nodded his understanding, letting it stand and a tacit agreement. "Good enough." It was more than he'd thought he would achieve.

"The heroic veterans of these two current wars are the unfortunate victims of the modern internet and the previous administration's rush to publicly declare victories and heroes," Burnett said with a sad shake of his head.

Kellan was genuinely baffled. "Could you please clarify that for me?"

"Before the war in Afghanistan was even twelve months old, a Marine was killed during a successful assault. His identity was released and a story came to light that a professional athlete walked away from a lucrative contract in order to serve his country. He was lauded as a hero - and he was - and his sacrifice was held up as an example to everyone. And then it came to light that his death was needless and senseless. Killed by friendly fire because an officer couldn't accurately call in an airstrike."

Kellan nodded, remembering the anger and a mother's tears.

"You remember when the Army supply truck was ambushed during the invasion of Baghdad, I'm sure?" Burnett continued. "You were in theater when it happened."

"My men and I were leading the Republican Guard on a merry chase all over Southern Iraq," Kellan acknowledged.

"You remember what they told you had happened to the captured female soldier?" Burnett asked. "They told you all how badly she'd been treated, how the Iraqi people had risked their own lives to tell Marines where she was so she could be rescued. The video footage of her rescue was released for broadcast and the Marines were declared heroes."

"It was a great boost for our moral, I remember," Kellan replied, the memories of that time in the desert, with Jonah at his side, played out across his mind. "It wasn't long before we realized those Marines weren't wearing the insignia of the team who had affected her rescue. When the soldier finally gave an interview, she said all of her injuries were sustained during the ambush and that she'd been treated well by her captors."

Burnett nodded. "And she wasn't rescued. She was voluntarily turned over by her captors." The Secretary snorted a derisive laugh. "As soon as you guys got to Baghdad, the President showed up in the war zone, declaring victory and that the conflict was over. Now, here we are, eight years later, and the new President is extracting our troops before the region is truly secure."

Kellan and everyone else on the ground in Iraq had known that speech was bullshit. They'd been months, if not years away from ending the conflict, even if it had been handled appropriately from the start. "I'm not sure how all of this applies to the awarding, or the refusal to award medals to the troops fighting the battles."

"The internet cannot be controlled, Kellan," Burnett answered. "There is an unspoken fear that the Medal of Honor will be awarded today, and tomorrow, the recipient will post a video on Facebook, showing himself and his buddies pissing on a stack of Qurans."

For Kellan, the pieces began to slot into place.

"It's not enough, anymore, to dress you guys up in your uniforms, trot you out and have you sell war bonds," Burnett continued with a note of regret. "The public expects the daily character of its war heroes to meet the same standard as their character in combat. You and I both know, that isn't always the case. And that kind of information can no longer be controlled by the military spin doctors. So, the way to avoid the embarrassment is to not award the medals in the first place."

Kellan wondered if the Secretary regretted that times had changed, or that the old guard still held sway. "I'm not sure how I feel about that, Cal."

"I don't think you should be very happy about it," Burnett replied heatedly. "And I'll tell you this, if you can find a way around that concern so that I can award more Medals of Honor, I'll do it."

That heartened Kellan significantly. "What does this all have to do with Sergeant Restrepo?"

"You're aware he was a Colombian national?" the Secretary asked after a sip of coffee.

"Yes. He enlisted in the Marines the same day he was granted his green card." Hirata had been careful to verify Restrepo's legal resident alien status in the early days of their investigation.

"That's correct. All reports indicate that his family fled death squads because his father refused to pay protection. He was a small-time activist and spoke out publicly against corruption." Burnett sat back in his chair and steepled his fingers. "What do you suppose the reaction would be if someone suddenly appeared on the internet accusing Restrepo's father of fleeing because he'd double crossed his fellow death squad members?"

The full picture finally came into focus for Kellan. "I think I understand, Cal. Thank you for your time and your candor."

Burnett stood and came around the end of his desk. "You're welcome, Kellan. It's been an honor to meet you."

Kellan stopped at the office door and turned to meet Burnett's eyes. "I have your word that you're open to awarding more Medals of Honor if I can ensure the DOD won't be embarrassed down the road?"

"Yes, you have my word." Burnett sealed their deal with a handshake.

As Jonah drove them back to their offices, Kellan recounted the entire conversation.

"So, what's your next step?" asked Jonah.

"I think we have to prove that Restrepo is worthy to receive the MOH," Kellan replied. "Then we parlay that into making the larger cases we want to make. I need to strategize with everyone, though." Ideas were racing through Kellan's mind, questions he needed to ask his staff.

Jonah was silent for several minutes before he sighed heavily. "I have the sinking feeling I'm not getting laid tonight."

Kellan laughed, not surprised that the tightness that had built up in his chest bled away.

Chapter 7

They were so wrapped up in the information spread out on the table before them, they hadn't bothered to change clothes when they'd arrived home. They'd gotten as far as removing their suit coats. Kellan stood now, rolling up his shirtsleeves but Jonah was still perfectly unwrinkled in his olive uniform trousers and khaki tie and shirt.

At some point, it had made sense for the rest of Kellan's staff to pursue the case of systemic discrimination in the awards process. They would compile what Kellan would need to report to the Senate. That left Jonah and Kellan to figure out why Sergeant Miguel Restrepo was being denied the Medal of Honor, and exactly by whom.

Kellan had been hungry for awhile, but each time he was about to call for a break to fix dinner, Jonah would connect another piece of the puzzle. Kellan ended up typing information into his notes, tagging document files and moving items into different folders on his hard drive.

Jonah stood at the long end of the table looking over the paperwork he had stacked and organized as he'd worked his way through the complicated mess. He balanced all of his weight on one leg, bent the knee of his second leg, and fisted his hands on his narrow hips. Jonah's handsome brow was marred by a frown of concentration as his intelligent blue eyes darted from photos to written reports. Jonah was tall and lean, built like he was made to wear the uniforms of the Marine Corps, and Kellan found him sexy as hell.

He may not have left the Corps so that he could explore a physical relationship with Jonah, but it had certainly gone in the 'pros' column when he'd been weighing his options.

"You're staring at me," Jonah said suddenly, startling Kellan out of his reverie, but not looking away from the organized chaos of their dining room table.

"Uh huh," Kellan replied, not at all ashamed at being called out.

"Staring at me isn't going to help us figure out why Restrepo is being blocked from receiving the MOH." Jonah finally looked Kellan in the eye.

"No, but it's a damn fun thing to do." Kellan smiled. He decided he was done with work for the night. Dinner first, then crawling into bed with Jonah were the only two things left on his agenda for the night.

Jonah snorted a laugh, one corner of his mouth lifting in the smile that always made Kellan's stomach twist in ways it embarrassed him to describe. "If you keep looking at me like that, we won't get back this tonight."

"Yeah, well, there's always tomorrow." Kellan grinned, openly flirting, and saved and closed all of his secure files. He stood from his chair and moved into the warm circle of Jonah's arms.

"You haven't gotten tired of having me under foot twenty-four-seven, yet?" Jonah asked, running is palms over Kellan's back. The question seemed casual, even humorous, but Kellan suspected that was a diversionary tactic.

"Not at all," Kellan replied with conviction. "You don't regret taking an office job, do you? Not wishing you'd promoted to Master Sergeant and stayed with a combat unit?"

"No," Jonah replied so quickly, Kellan nearly doubted him. "I hate having to wear the service uniform – fucking ties – but I like using my brain this much. This is important work, too. This matters."

"I'm glad you think so," Kellan said quietly against the warm skin of Jonah's throat, relief washing through him. He inhaled and caught the scent of the cologne Jonah had begun to wear. He hadn't asked but Kellan assumed Jonah had never worn cologne regularly because he spent so much time getting sweaty, dirty, or just plain wet. Marines were amphibious, after all.

"Are you coming to the same conclusion I am, about all of this?" Jonah's question confused Kellan momentarily.

It took several moments to realize Jonah was referring to the issue with Restrepo. "Probably, but what conclusion are you reaching?"

"Someone has been lying about what happened inside that house in Fallujah," Jonah replied. "We might need to conduct our own interviews."

Kellan had been coming to that conclusion over the last several days, yes. He was still hoping to find a way around it. "If we want to continue pursuing this; if we want the truth, regardless of what that truth is, I believe that is what we're going to have to do."

Jonah made a frustrated sound. "Send someone else, this time." It sounded almost like a plea.

"I'm not sending anyone to do something I'm not willing to do myself." Did Jonah expect anything else from him?

"Yeah, I know," Jonah replied with resignation. "I'm going with you, you know."

"You *are* my military aide." Kellan pulled back to meet Jonah's eyes. They were standing in the dining room of a small house in Virginia, casually discussing the fact they were going to have to head directly into a war zone.

Kellan sighed inwardly. Always a Marine.

"Don't get kidnapped this time," Jonah said in mock annoyance.

"Why not? It was such a fun experience the first time."

Jonah rolled his eyes. Kellan laughed.

"I'm getting out of this monkey suit," Jonah said, heading for the bedroom and stripping off his uniform tie.

"Oh, hey, wait for me!" Kellan chased after Jonah. "I want to help!"

• • • •

KELLAN WAS A LITTLE more superstitious than he liked to admit. When the universe kept aligning in such a way to either thwart or facilitate something he wanted to accomplish, it was difficult not to be.

When Senator Gilchrist had told Kellan to get to Camp Pendleton to start re-interviewing the Marines involved in the battle that had taken Sergeant Restrepo's life, Jonah had coordinated the logistics of the trip. Neither of them had been aware that they were arriving just in time for the 2nd Annual Recon Challenge. They couldn't have manufactured a better cover.

"Jonah?"

They both turned at the sound of Jonah's name.

Jonah's features split into a grin. "Yarwood," he greeted, extending his hand.

Corporal Corey Yarwood approached, dressed in full utilities including the eight cornered, billed cover. He'd changed since Kellan had last seen him. Corey was the same height, but he held himself a little taller. He seemed broader in the chest and shoulders. Two years had matured Corey, that much was obvious. He'd still been boyish, when Kellan had met him. Now, he was unquestionably all man.

Corey grasped Jonah's hand and shook it briskly. They pulled each other in for the ultra-masculine, back-slapping hug of the alpha male. Corey was smiling wide when he stepped back, his eyes shone as he looked up into Jonah's face. He released Jonah's hand but now stood gripping his bicep.

"I had no idea you were coming in for this!" Corey exclaimed. "Why didn't you email me?"

"It was last minute and I didn't think about it," Jonah replied. "You remember Kellan, of course," he said, reaching back and gesturing Kellan forward.

Kellan's brain was processing what he was observing. Corey's open, flushed expression of joy, his brightly shining eyes as he stared up at Jonah. The implication was just sinking in when Kellan stepped forward to shake Corey's hand. He watched Corey's smile falter, his eyes shutter as he took Kellan's hand.

"Of course I do," he said politely. His grip on Kellan's hand was firm, his gaze direct, but his greeting lacked the enthusiasm of the one he'd given Jonah. "It's good to see you again, sir."

Oh, but it wasn't. How had Kellan missed that before? "It's a pleasure to see you again, Corey," Kellan said genuinely. "I often inquire after you, it's good to see for myself that Jonah's reports are accurate."

Kellan didn't blame Corey for his crush on Jonah. He understood it better than anyone. It just saddened him that it would probably always make things awkward between them. Kellan wondered if Jonah knew.

Corey appeared taken aback at Kellan's words. "Th-thank you, sir. I appreciate your interest in my well being."

"Please, call me Kellan." He gripped Corey's bicep in a friendly gesture. "It's the weekend and we're here informally. Besides, I'm out of Corps."

Corey blinked. "That's...not exactly why people call you sir, sir."

Jonah chuckled. "I keep telling him that and he doesn't seem to get it." He gripped Corey's neck affectionately. "So, why aren't you competing today, Corporal Yarwood?"

"We got word that First Recon is deploying again in nine months." Corey grew serious. "I didn't need the additional stress in my life."

"Christ. You deployed two years ago," Jonah growled.

"And by the time I deploy again it will be three," Corey said with a shrug. "I think I've been stateside this long because I kept getting accepted into training classes."

"What are you up to now?" Kellan asked. "You did Mountain Warfare, Survival, and Jump School, right?"

"Affirmative, sir, uh, Kellan." Corey flushed slightly and folded his arms over his chest. "If I make Sergeant before we deploy, I might get to go as a Team Leader."

Jonah held up a hand and he and Corey bumped fists. Kellan chuckled, but he couldn't help being impressed. Corey was moving up in rank quickly, much the way Jonah had. If he survived his upcoming deployment, he'd most likely return with a chest full of medals, also like Jonah.

"Are you guys here just for the Challenge?" Corey inquired.

Jonah glanced at Kellan. Kellan held his gaze for a heartbeat before looking away. Jonah knew Corey better than he did and he had good judgment. If he thought it was wise to read Corey in, Kellan had no objection.

"We're here on a special mission," Jonah replied. "And what I tell you goes no further."

"You have my word, Jonah," Corey said solemnly.

Kellan listened to Jonah explain Kellan's work for the Senate, and how they were looking into the denied medal for Sergeant Restrepo's valor during the Second Battle of Fallujah.

"Yeah, it's kind of shitty that no one will take the word of the Marines who were there," Corey said.

"Does your Platoon Sergeant ever talk about it?" Jonah asked smoothly.

"No." Corey shook his head emphatically. "If I hadn't seen the ribbon on his uniform, I would never know he won the Silver Star."

"If I told you that we have good reason to believe that one of the Marines who was there, one of the Marines who has given testimony regarding Restrepo's worthiness for the Medal of Honor, has been lying about the events of that day, would you suspect your Platoon Sergeant?" Jonah's question was carefully worded and quietly asked.

Corey stared hard at Jonah for several interminable moments. "No," he finally answered. "No, I wouldn't suspect Staff Sergeant Gilman of lying. I would expect that he's told the truth as he knows it to be."

"That's an interesting distinction," Kellan said without thinking.

"The fog of war can affect our perceptions," Corey responded placidly. "Combat is chaotic by nature. Just because someone is present at a particular battle doesn't mean he has firsthand knowledge of every detail. When you were snatched in Diyala, Kellan, I didn't know who had been dragged into the Range Rover, I just knew it was an American and I was damn well gonna fight."

"And I've never gotten to say thank you for slowing them down long enough for Jonah to be able to track their retreat," Kellan said. "How's your head, these days?"

Corey's fingers lifted to his temple in what looked like an unconscious gesture. "I have a pretty good scar but beyond that, I healed up fine."

"I'm glad to hear that," Kellan said and turned back to watch the kids climbing the simulated rock wall. Corey would probably be more candid with Jonah than he would with Kellan.

"What does the platoon think of Gilman in general?" Jonah asked.

"He's pretty well respected," replied Corey. "He knows his shit. He's no Jonah Carver, though."

Jonah made an obscene sound. "Is he the kind of Marine who would lie to cover for another Marine?"

"If by cover you mean deflect blame onto himself to protect a Marine in his command, it's possible," said Corey. "If by cover you mean lying to hide something wrong another Marine did, I doubt it."

There was silence and Kellan suspected Jonah had found out what he wanted to know. Minutes later, the conversation became about who was competing, what their chances were, and reminiscing about their time together in Diyala Province.

The day turned fun and relaxing. By the time the winner of the Challenge was announced, Corey seemed as comfortable with Kellan as he did with Jonah, even if his eyes shined just a little brighter when he looked at Jonah.

When Kellan announced he was ready to head to the hotel, Jonah shook Corey's hand again.

"We'll get a beer before I have to leave," he said, gripping Corey's shoulder one last time before he stepped away.

"I'd like that, Jonah," Corey said, seeming at peace finally. "Talk to you later, Kellan."

"Have a good night, Corey." Kellan made sure Corey was out of sight before he slid his hand into the back pocket of Jonah's jeans.

• • • •

"STAFF SERGEANT TRENT Gilman?" Jonah asked as the Marine entered the small office where they were conducting the interviews.

"That's correct, First Sergeant Carver," Gilman replied. He shook Kellan's hand firmly when Jonah introduced him.

Since they were interviewing NCOs, all of whom Jonah outranked, they decided Jonah would ask the questions. It was likely to feel less confrontational that way, which meant they could possibly get more truthful answers.

"We're not rehashing Sergeant Restrepo's worthiness for the Medal of Honor," Jonah explained. "We're investigating why a Marine so obviously worthy has been denied the Medal twice, despite the public support."

"I admit, Top, I don't like my testimony being disregarded like it has been," Gilman said candidly as they all three settled into chairs.

"I don't blame you," Jonah commiserated. "I wouldn't either." He scrolled through a document on the screen of his tablet. "Just walk me through the events, from beginning to end, in your own words. If I have questions, I'll ask them afterward."

Gilman recounted how he and his patrol had been going house-to-house, searching for armed insurgents. It was the Second Battle of Fallujah and they were outnumbered, only beginning the surge that would eventually take the city back.

They came under heavy fire and took refuge in a bombed out house while they dug in, regrouped, and prepared to take the fight to the enemy. A Marine made his way to the roof and was hit. When he came falling down the stairs, two more Marines went up, both of whom were hit but still managed to toss grenades and return fire.

The two Marines on the roof held the insurgents off, preventing them from identifying targets to shoot and from making entry into the house. As the rest of the team took cover in the outer rooms, insurgents managed to launch grenades into the house. The Marines were taken out one-by-one and had to pull back further into the house. Gilman himself had shrapnel wounds in his legs and crawled into the room in time to see Restrepo, bleeding from a head wound, helping a quickly fading Gunnery Sergeant John Warner, stumble in and fall.

An insurgent grenade bounced off a wall and rolled into the room where they had all taken cover. It came to rest just feet from where Restrepo and Warner lay wounded. Gilman watched Restrepo throw himself over the now-limp body of Gunny Warner. Restrepo's body absorbed the blast and the shrapnel from the exploding grenade. Gilman had been far enough away the shrapnel missed him, embedding in nearby walls.

Sergeant Restrepo was shredded by shrapnel and he was dead by the time the corpsman reached them. Gunny Warner survived, but eventually lost a leg below the knee.

"They said the medical board that reviewed the forensics determined that Restrepo's head wound was too severe, he didn't have the conscious thought or physical ability to cover Gunny's body with his own," said Gilman. "That's bullshit, Top. I saw it with my own eyes." He was vehement in his declaration, leaning toward Jonah slightly.

"What was Gunny Warner doing when the grenade landed in the room?" Jonah asked. In his typical fashion, Jonah's posture appeared relaxed, but Kellan saw the focus and intensity in his eyes.

"Gunny was already unconscious," Gilman answered. "He'd been shot up pretty bad and was losing a lot of blood."

Kellan focused on Gilman's last sentence and could tell from the set of Jonah's shoulders, he'd picked up on it, as well. There had been hints of this in other documents. Kellan had never been able to find an official statement that mentioned Restrepo having gunshot wounds. Not even the final medical reports mentioned anything other than blast and fragmentation wounds.

"So, there's no chance he pulled an already unconscious Restrepo on top of himself as a shield?" Jonah pressed.

"No." Gilman gave an emphatic shake of his head. "Me and Lance Corporal Rich Connell saw the same thing as we were crawling into the room."

"Gunny and Restrepo were fragged. Gunny Warner was unconscious when another grenade landed in the room. Sergeant Restrepo threw himself over Gunny's body, absorbing the majority of the blast and the shrapnel," Jonah summarized. "Is that it?"

Sergeant Gilman nodded. "At some point, they both took gunshot wounds, too."

Kellan tensed. He shifted in his chair slightly, to mask his urge to leap up and press for answers.

Jonah frowned slightly, as he scanned through the scrolling screen on his tablet. Kellan knew it was for show, so he waited to see if Jonah's tactic would pay off. "When did they take rounds?" Jonah asked. "If the insurgents hadn't breached the house and only the roof was taking small arms fire, when did they take rounds? If all of you were pulling back to avoid grenades, and they were both down when the insurgents breached the house, when were they shot?"

"It happened before we all met up in that room so I didn't see what happened," Gilman answered without hesitation. "That's why it was never part of my testimony. It shouldn't matter anyway. Restrepo sacrificed himself to save Gunny. I saw him do it, Top. He was a hero that day, no matter what happened before that grenade got tossed in."

"You know what you saw, Sergeant," Jonah replied noncommittally. "And it's consistent with the Silver Star citation. Who was still in the room Restrepo and Warner had fled? Do you recall?"

The Sergeant paused, obviously scanning his memory of the event. "I *think* it was Staff Sergeant Galen Foster, but I'm not real sure."

"That's okay. It's listed somewhere in one of the reports," Jonah replied casually. He and Kellan both knew for a fact it had been Foster in that room. "Okay. I think we're done here," he declared as he rose and shook Gilman's hand. "If we have more questions we'll let your CO know."

When Gilman was gone, Jonah and Kellan resumed their seats. "What's our next move, sir?" Jonah asked.

"First, I want to interview Lance Corporal Rich Connell and verify his story matches Gilman's," Kellan said, scrolling the screen of his own tablet. "Once we've done that, we need to interview Gunnery Sergeant Galen Foster. All accounts, including his own, state that he was in the outer room with Warner and Restrepo when they started taking grenades."

"It's looking more and more like a case of friendly fire," Jonah confirmed. "And someone arranged for a medical panel to provide a finding that would disqualify Restrepo for the MOH, without pointing a finger at anyone for lighting up a fellow Marine."

"This entire thing is so FUBAR," Kellan said, his anger burning hot and knotting his gut. "False medical findings have most likely been released to the family and the public. We need to figure out how to get our hands on the real reports, including photos, and determine who they're protecting and why."

"Who is *they*?" Jonah asked in bafflement.

"I have no idea, that's a piece of the larger puzzle," Kellan answered.

Jonah rubbed a thumb and forefinger over his eyes. Subtle bags had formed that Kellan hadn't seen on Jonah since those first days of Operation Iraqi Freedom. "You know Foster is in Afghanistan, right?" Jonah asked.

"Yep." Kellan had wondered how long Jonah would wait to have this conversation.

"You know I want you to send someone else to interview him, right?" Jonah met Kellan's eyes, expression resigned.

"Yep." There was no one to send besides Jonah, and Kellan wasn't letting him go alone. They sat in tense silence for several interminable moments.

"You know I'm going with you, right?" Jonah finally asked.

"We discussed this already," Kellan said with a tired grin. Whatever else they were both feeling, Jonah's concern warmed him. "I don't want you back in a war zone any more than you want me in one. We'll go together, so we can at least watch one another's backs."

"Just don't make me have to chase you through the streets of a hostile city again," Jonah said as he stood and headed for the exit.

"If you insist," Kellan joked as he followed Jonah out the door.

Chapter 8

Jonah whistled the opening bars of the theme song to 'Welcome Back Kotter' and Kellan couldn't quite stifle all of his laughter. It had taken many weeks, some stern words from Senator Gilchrist, and finally a private meeting between the Senator and Secretary Burnett. Kellan wasn't privy to what had been said in that meeting, but the Secretary had finally relented and approved Kellan and Jonah to fly to Camp Leatherneck in order to interview Gunnery Sergeant Galen Foster.

"I admit, I didn't think we were going to get clearance to come here," Jonah said, his breath warm on Kellan's cheek as he leaned over his shoulder to watch their descent.

"Honestly, neither did I," Kellan concurred, admiring the stark beauty of the Afghan countryside. "Secretary Burnett is keeping his word and facilitating Hammond's and Giammona's investigation, but he has solidly stonewalled us."

"Which means there's something there to find," Jonah concluded darkly.

"Mmm." The 747 banked and the sprawling features of Camp Leatherneck came into view.

Designed to accommodate 20,000 Marines, Camp Leatherneck was a combination of single-story, pre-fabricated structures and beige colored tents. Marines slept on cots, twenty to a tent or 2,000 to a structure. As austere as it was, it had been built up extensively since its establishment just a few short years before. The 3,282 yard runway they were currently landing on was just one of the new and improved features.

Jonah stood and retrieved their bags from the overhead bins. He pulled their sidearms from inside the bags and handed Kellan's to him. All through the cabin, passengers were donning holsters and handguns.

Their flight had originated at Ramstein Air Base in Germany, so all passengers were military or CIA.

With their nine millimeter Berettas secured in their thigh holsters, Kellan followed Jonah down the stairs of the plane. Jonah paused to place his utility cover on his head. He was dressed in his desert cammo diggis - MARPAT utilities.

Kellan had worn and packed the most practical civvies he could find. Cotton tee-shirts, light-weight, long sleeved cotton shirts to protect from the sun, Carhart canvas pants and beige lug soled boots. He pulled his Padres ball cap down over his eyes and slid on his sunglasses. Jonah called his shades 'snivel gear', but Kellan just smiled in response.

"Would you be Mr. Kellan Reynolds, sir?" asked a corporal as he stood at the bottom of the stairs.

"I am," Kellan replied, stepping onto the Tarmac. "My aide, First Sergeant Jonah Carver."

"First Sergeant," the corporal greeted with a nod. "I'm Corporal Ruhl. I've been tasked with escorting you to meet with the base commander, Colonel Chuck Mills."

"Lead the way, Corporal." Kellan fell into step beside the young Marine, Jonah close on his six.

"I trust you had a pleasant flight, sir?" Ruhl asked politely.

"We did, thank you. Is this your first deployment?" Kellan had mastered the art of small talk long ago.

"No, sir, my second," Ruhl replied. "When I complete this one, I hope to be accepted into BRC."

Kellan nodded. The corporal knew exactly who he and Jonah were. "Good luck with that. I'm sure you'd make an excellent Recon Marine."

Activity was peaking inside the camp perimeter. Marines bustled around, some wearing combat gear and carrying weapons, obviously preparing to head out on a patrol. Others wore Under Armor fleece shirts or diggi uniform blouses as the conducted in-camp business. There was a tension in the air, a constant sense of readiness that felt vaguely familiar to Kellan. His time serving in Afghanistan had been during the opening months of OEF and they had all had such conviction and enthusiasm, nearly a decade ago.

The bright sun reflected off of all the light colored structures was blinding and Kellan was grateful for his sun glasses, snivel gear or not. Despite the sun, the temperature wasn't as warm as Kellan had expected. He knew from experience the nights got cold. So cold that it seeped into his bones took up residence, no matter how many layers of bedding he rolled up in.

The paths between camp facilities were all hard-packed and well-worn from the passing of many booted feet. Everything around them was coated in a layer of fine, power-like dust, the same pale beige as the endless sands that surrounded them.

"Damn moon dust gets into everything," Corporal Ruhl muttered.

"Excuse me?" Kellan asked.

"The top most layer of sand is this fine, powdery stuff we call moon dust," Ruhl said. "It gets picked up easy by the wind and gets into everything. We can't keep anything clean for very long."

Reaching a large, neutral colored structure, Ruhl held the door open for Kellan and Jonah. Colonel Mills was a short, stout, graying man with a stern expression.

"You're here to speak with Gunnery Sergeant Galen Foster," Mills confirmed.

"That's correct, Colonel," Kellan replied, trying to get a quick read on Mills.

"Foster is with Charlie Company, Third Battalion, Second Marines." The Colonel pointed to a map hung on the wall behind his desk. "Charlie is currently staffing a combat operations post sixty klicks from here."

Kellan's annoyance rose. He wondered if Foster had been assigned to the post before or *after* this trip had been approved. "That's rather problematic."

"It would be, except for two things," Mills said. "First, Top Carver functioning as your aide bolsters your personal security. Second, you aren't the typical civilian. Golf Company is scheduled for a patrol tomorrow, and Charlie Company's COP is on their list of contacts to make."

"That sounds fortuitous," Kellan said noncommittally, just in case he was reading the Colonel wrong.

Mills folded his arms over his chest and looked from Kellan to Jonah and back again. "If you're up for it, I'm not opposed to letting you accompany Golf Company on their patrol. You can conduct your interview tomorrow and be on a plane back to Germany the day after."

Kellan was pleasantly surprised that the Colonel so easily facilitated his mission. Maybe it was more than just the enlisted ranks who were unhappy that Restrepo had twice been denied the MOH. "That is an acceptable plan, Colonel."

• • • •

TO KELLAN'S ANNOYANCE, he needed Jonah's help with his MTV – modular tactical vest – just before they stepped off on patrol. It was different from the interceptor body armor that had been standard when Kellan had been an officer. Luckily, the Kevlar helmet hadn't changed.

As they approached the line of Humvees swarming with young Marines, the captain broke off from his men and approached Jonah and Kellan.

"Captain, sir," Jonah greeted, "First Sergeant Jonah Carver."

"Top." The Captain's name patch read Miller.

"May I introduce Kellan Reynolds." Jonah gestured in Kellan's direction.

Captain Miller shook his hand briskly. "I'm honored to have you both with us today," Miller said in a serious tone. "I don't even mind that you're both armed. At least I know neither of you will cause yourselves or one of my men harm with a negligent discharge." His small grin took some of the edge from his words. "But if things go tits up, the two of you will take cover in the Humvee. How copy?"

"Solid, sir," Jonah replied, still standing stiffly, every inch the enlisted Marine.

"Solid copy, Captain," Kellan said emphatically. They'd proven themselves in combat enough to have lost count. He and Jonah wanted to make out intact, they had no issue with taking cover and staying safe.

"I know you're both very capable, but you haven't trained with the Marines in my company," Miller continued. "They have a shorthand and a rhythm that you take the chance of disrupting."

"Absolutely understood, Captain Miller," Kellan assured him. "I was a platoon commander, I clearly remember what it was like to have a cohesively functioning team. We're armed for our own protection, not for the purposes of joining in combat."

"If one of you comes face to face with an insurgent, by all means, put a bullet in his brain," the captain said. "Otherwise, stay behind cover and follow any and all directions my men give you."

"You have my word, Captain," Kellan agreed. If Kellan was honest with himself, he was even a little bit rusty when it came to combat.

Jonah and Kellan were assigned to ride in the rear seats of a Humvee in the center of the convoy. Kellan had ridden through Iraq in a gun truck, which was less cramped and more open, so he wasn't used to the claustrophobic feel.

"Is the view different from the back seats?" he asked Jonah jokingly.

As an NCO and a Team Leader, Jonah had spent his deployments in the front passenger seat.

"All the additional armor changed the view after that first deployment," Jonah responded. "For all the reduced visibility and reduced maneuverability caused by the hillbilly armor, we might as well be in tanks instead of Humvees."

Their conversation was interrupted by the roar of the diesel engine firing up. Their gunner climbed up the rungs of the small ladder into the turret on the roof. The familiar sound of a fifty caliber round being racked into place reached Kellan's ears.

Minutes later, they were oscar-mike. The rough, unpaved roads made the ride kidney-jarring and uncomfortable. The volume of the engine made idle chatter with Jonah impractical and getting to know the other Marines in the victor impossible. Kellan settled in for a long, boring journey of staring out the window.

The patrol's first stop was at the fields of a local farmer. The man greeted Captain Miller and the rest of his family soon joined them. The conversation was friendly and animated, rapidly translated by one of the Marines.

Their Humvee's Team Leader advised them it was clear for Jonah and Kellan to exit the Humvee, but not to wander too far. They were told to extend their situational awareness and keep their heads on swivels. This farmer was friendly but insurgents were everywhere.

Kellan walked along the side of the rutted road that paralleled the farmer's crops. Jonah stayed right on Kellan's six but didn't say much. Kellan blinked several times, his brain refusing to register what it was he was seeing. Granted, this was the first time he'd ever seen this particular crop outside of a photograph.

They stood looking out over acres and acres of infamous Afghan poppy plants.

Coming to a stop, Kellan quietly asked Jonah, "Are you aware of what this is?"

Jonah seemed to focus on a plant just a few feet from where they stood. "Is it what I think it is?"

"Poppies," Kellan replied. He should have recognized them sooner. Now that he looked, he could see the score marks where the farmer had let the sap ooze.

"Stay close to me, Kel," Jonah said tightly, his body going tense as he turned three-sixty. "He's growing this for a local tribal leader who could show up at any time."

Kellan didn't argue. He knew Jonah was right. "We probably shouldn't separate ourselves from the rest of the Marines."

Together they walked back toward their Humvee, mixing among the Marines who stood watch and held the perimeter. Captain Miller was still talking to the farmer and it seemed a friendly, informative conversation. Kellan approached slowly, ready to be waved off by Miller if necessary.

Instead, Miller gestured Kellan forward. He introduced them both to the old farmer, saying that Jonah and Kellan were honored guests, on their way to talk about a Marine who had died a hero.

The translator went through the polite ritual greetings.

"Wasim cultivates poppies at the *request* of a local tribal leader," Captain Miller explained. "He would rather not, but it's a crop that pays well enough for his family to live comfortably."

"Not to mention the fact that cooperating with the tribal leader allows him to live in relative peace and safety," Kellan added.

"It bothers Wasim that he is a source for something that makes so many American people ill, but he has to take care of his family," Miller said. "The tribal leader might be able to force Wasim to cultivate the crop, but he hasn't earned Wasim's loyalty."

"He provides Marines with information?" Kellan asked.

"He's very cooperative," the captain said with a nod. "In the past, Wasim has given us information on both the activities of the tribal leader, and the movements of strangers coming into the area."

"Insurgents?" Kellan asked in surprise.

"As it turned out, yes," Miller confirmed. "But as Wasim said, strangers are uncommon in this region. They're easily noticed and typically not functioning with innocent intent."

"Has Wasim been compensated for this information?" Kellan asked.

"Not directly," the captain said quickly. "Not in a quid-pro-quo arrangement. But we have assisted him to recover missing livestock, we've helped him make repairs when irrigation levees have broken, and when a herd of goats went missing, we saw to it they were replaced."

"Hearts and minds?" Kellan smiled.

"Hearts and minds."

The translator expressed all of their farewells to Wasim and the Marines climbed back into their victors. Their next stop was at a combat post, which was nothing more than a platoon of Marines dug into a flat patch of dirt and rock. Even now, Marines were squaring walls of trenches with e-tools and stacking sandbags.

"Ammo restock, looks like," Jonah mused.

"MREs, too," Kellan said, as he watched crates and cartons get tossed and stacked.

Their stop was brief and they were oscar-mike again.

Kellan was sure his spine was permanently compressed by the time they reached the combat post that was Gunnery Sergeant Galen Foster's current billet. As soon as the compound gate secured behind them and the Marines began to exit their victors, Kellan carefully stepped out and stretched his aching muscles.

This COP was in what appeared to be some sort of ancient fortification. Tall walls made of mud brick encircled the entire compound. Two single-story structures stood side-by-side, also made of mud brick. The original wooden roof had been reinforced with more secure metals, not unlike the hillbilly armor of the Humvees. It was primitive and austere, only slightly less spartan than the first COP they had visited.

Activity buzzed around them. Marines wearing Under Armor shirts unloaded trucks, cleaned weapons, and worked under the hoods of vehicles. Kellan heard laughter and swearing, dirty jokes and most of all, complaining. Marines loved to complain.

Captain Miller took Kellan and Jonah to meet the post commander who quickly summoned Gunnery Sergeant Foster. It didn't take the Gunny long to respond since he wasn't on watch. The post commander showed them to a small, cramped, windowless room where Jonah and Kellan could talk with Foster privately.

The room contained several backless camp chairs and empty crates stood on end to serve as tables. Jonah arranged three stools equidistance apart but still close together. Kellan would use proximity to turn up the pressure during this conversation. Foster held the key to something, they were convinced. Kellan just wasn't sure what that key would unlock.

"How can I be of help, sirs?" Foster asked, unable to mask his anxiety.

"A Senate committee has put me in charge of determining why next to no veterans of Operations Iraqi Freedom and Enduring Freedom are being awarded the Medal of Honor," Kellan informed him brusquely, falling silent to gauge Foster's reaction.

The Gunny looked stricken for the briefest of moments before he schooled his features. "What does that have to do with me, sirs?"

"You know what it has to do with you, Gunnery Sergeant," Kellan replied sharply. "Sergeant Restrepo has twice been denied the MOH and you are on record as a witness to his act of valor."

"But I'm on record as supporting Sergeant Restrepo," Foster said in confusion. "How can I be responsible for him not receiving the medal?"

"I didn't say you were," Kellan said mildly. "Secondary to that investigation, the First Sergeant and I have determined there are certain inconsistencies in the story of Restrepo's heroism. They don't affect the current status of the Sergeant's medal, but they are problematic on their own."

"Marines have lied, Gunnery Sergeant," Jonah interjected sharply. "Not about Restrepo's heroism, but about why he had to take heroic action at all."

Foster's posture stiffened and his expression shuttered.

Kellan leaned toward Foster, resting his forearms on his knees. "Now, the fact he was awarded the Silver Star means that investigators uncovered the truth about what happened that day, and Restrepo's actions have been verified and validated. What I want to know is who the investigators are covering up for, and why?"

Foster swallowed audibly. He shifted slightly in his chair, eyes darting between Kellan and Jonah.

Kellan sighed in frustration. "Do you want me to run down the list of the other Marines who were in the house and how I know none of them are who is being protected? Or can we just cut to the chase?"

Foster cleared his throat. "Do you I need to retain military counsel, sir?"

Kellan sat back in his chair. He'd been firing for effect, gauging how he needed to adjust is aim. Now it seemed he'd had good effect on target from the start. "You tell me? Have you had to retain counsel before?"

"It was a mistake, sir, an accident," Foster blurted. "They said I could be disciplined but there were no grounds for a Court Martial."

Kellan glanced at Jonah and found he was looking at Kellan. They had already determined this much on their own, none of this was coming as any surprise.

"Gunnery Sergeant, I don't give a shit about a case of accidental friendly fire," Kellan said dialing in the aim of his shot. "Your actions do not diminish Sergeant Restrepo's valor. What I *do* give a shit about is that a hero is being denied the Medal of Honor because of your mistake. Sergeant Restrepo is dead, denied an award he's worthy of, and here you are, promoted to Gunnery Sergeant. That right there, Foster, pisses me off."

"The promotion wasn't part of the deal," Foster declared, sounding desperate.

"What deal?" Kellan demanded, quelling is excitement, needing to keep digging toward the truth. "Even if your promotion wasn't part of a *deal*, there was no mention of any friendly fire incident in your fit-rep to prevent it."

Foster sat stiffly, shaking his head, refusing to make eye contact with either of them.

"Foster!" Jonah barked, using the command voice that had made many PFCs shake in their LPCs. "Mr. Reynolds made us fly all the way to Afghanistan to speak with you, because it was the quickest way to get right to the truth. If you don't tell him what he wants to know, he'll just go home and take his sweet time digging it up in safety and comfort."

"You can be assured my interest in this mystery is peaked," Kellan said, lifting an eyebrow at Foster's continued silence.

"Dammit." Foster's sudden expletive surprised Kellan, but he quickly masked it. "They said this wouldn't happen. They promised me no one would ever show up asking questions."

"Well, they didn't count on me," Kellan replied, smiling humorlessly. "I'm not a politician. I don't have a cushy government job I'm afraid of losing. I work for a company that is funded by private sources that expect me to rock boats and rattle cages."

"Sir, if I tell you who wanted this all to go away, it'll piss off some important people," Foster said pleadingly.

"The last time I wanted to know something that someone else wanted kept secret, I got kidnapped and beaten." Kellan used a matter-of-fact tone. "And still, here I am."

Foster sighed with resignation. "How much do you know about my family, sir?"

"If you mean am I aware of who your step-father is, yes," Kellan replied, struggling to make the necessary connections. Foster's step-father was a wealthy entrepreneur, with no ties to military contracts or even politics.

"His oldest son wants to run for public office in 2012." Foster held up his hands as if the rest was obvious.

"You're telling me your step-father bought everyone's silence, right up through the Department of Defense, so his son could run for political office?" Kellan confirmed. Even with the dots connected, the picture was far from clear.

"My step-brother expected to use me as a war hero in his campaign," Foster said, anger bleeding through. "He's still pissed at me for not finishing my degree so I could be commissioned. He was double pissed when he realized I'd been downgraded from hero to tarnished veteran."

"You're fucking kidding me?" Jonah sounded both angry and incredulous.

Foster shook his head slowly. "No, First Sergeant. I wish I was."

"There's no reason to think a case of accidental friendly fire involving a step-brother would damage his campaign," Kellan said, wondering how much of this to believe.

"He didn't want to be tainted by a step-brother who shot a Medal of Honor recipient. I think he even resents that I wasn't the one who qualified for the MOH. He wants to claim relation to a war hero, which means I'm going to be vetted during the campaign. So, he made anything un-hero-like just go away."

It was just outrageous enough, Kellan believed it was the truth. It also matched a lot of other facts he already had. "Sergeant Restrepo deserves to be awarded the Medal of Honor," he said, getting to his feet. "I'm going to do what I have to do to see that he does. I hope you're ready for what's about to happen. Even if you're not, I don't really give a shit."

Foster also stood. "I don't care, sir. I don't like living the lie. It's my family that's going to be pissed off."

"I think it's obvious I'm not concerned about that," Kellan replied, nonplussed. Kellan almost welcomed the fight. He hated this kind of political shit.

"Gunnery Sergeant, go advise your platoon commander we're done with you," Jonah said sharply. Kellan knew that whatever excuses Foster offered, Jonah held him responsible for going along with the deception.

In silence, Kellan and Jonah returned to their Humvee. Hopefully the platoon would be ready to step off soon.

"Can you believe this shit?" Jonah asked with disgust.

"I can, but it doesn't mean I like it," Kellan replied. He understood Jonah's reaction and shared it on a certain level.

They had to cool their heels for another ninety mikes. Jonah was agitated by the time Captain Miller ordered the platoon into their victors. Kellan struggled not to let Jonah's tension affect him, but it was difficult.

Back in his MTV and Kevlar, Kellan settled uncomfortably in his seat. He had a lot to think about, a lot to do when they got back stateside. He stared out the window at the flat, barren, unimpressive landscape. The platoon was scheduled to stop in a small village en route back to Leatherneck and that would break up the monotony somewhat.

Movement and a large cloud of dust caught Kellan's attention. He glanced back slightly and caught sight of two men on a small motorcycle, pacing their Humvee from several meters off the road. The hair on Kellan's neck and arms stood up. His skin felt sensitive and prickly. Reflexively, he reached for his M16, startled back to reality when he remembered he no longer had one.

"Staff Sergeant, we've got a motorcycle on our seven o'clock," Kellan shouted over the roar of the Humvee's engine. From the corner of his eye, he saw Jonah's head swivel around quickly.

"Yep, we're tracking it," the team leader in the front passenger seat replied over his shoulder. "No aggressive movements yet."

"Are we a likely target?" Jonah asked.

"We don't secure equipment to the outsides of the victors that they have an interest in stealing," the Staff Sergeant answered. "But a magnetized bomb on a less armored part of the Humvees is a serious threat."

Kellan turned back and watched the small motorcycle kick up a large plume of moon dust.

"There's always a chance they're from the village and are just waiting to see where we're headed," said the Staff Sergeant.

Kellan hoped so, but a glance at Jonah told him they both had their doubts.

The platoon pulled into the small, tribal village. One large structure stood at the far end of the main road, such as it was. Smaller structures dotted the immediate area, separated by narrow foot paths. Nothing was paved, everything was covered in the ubiquitous gritty sand and fine moon dust.

The victors came to a stop in the center of the main road, arranged in a herringbone pattern for easy access and quick egress if necessary. The Marines clambered out, immediately setting up a wide perimeter, M16s tucked to their shoulders, muzzles lowered. The gunners all stayed in their turrets, adjusting the ranges of their Fifty-cals and Mark-19s.

Immediately, children began to gather in clusters. They tried to engage the Marines in conversation with hand gestures and broken English. The platoon was friendly, but Kellan knew they had all extended their situational awareness.

Their team leader leaned in the window. "Captain Miller says the two of you are to stay put while we're here. Take advantage of the Humvee's armor."

"Understood, Staff Sergeant," Kellan acknowledged. He just hoped this was a quick stop.

"If we come under threat and it's no longer safe, some of us will come move you," the Staff Sergeant said and started to turn away.

"How long are we expected to be here?" Jonah asked as the team leader withdrew from the window. There he went again, reading Kellan's mind.

"An hour, unless we encounter trouble," replied the Staff Sergeant before he disappeared.

"Let's hope we don't encounter trouble," Jonah muttered under his breath.

The children were still gathered around but kept at a distance from the Humvees. A small number of women watched them warily as they went about their business. Young men gathered in groups, much like the children, and eyed the Marines with hostility.

Kellan's leg bounced violently. He'd been in situations like this before, many of them in downtown Baghdad. Except he'd been the one in command then, and he'd been outside of his victor and armed with his M16.

"I miss my M4," Jonah murmured.

Kellan was about to make a joke about mind reading when a sound caught his attention. The high-pitched whine of the motorcycle drifted from the distance. Closing his eyes and focusing, Kellan thought he detected it coming from their six.

He resisted the temptation to verify the Marines were aware of the motorcycle's proximity. He had to let them do their jobs.

"You guys hear that?" Kellan turned to see Jonah talking with a Marine just outside of his window. He looked casual and almost disinterested but Kellan felt the tension and aggression rolling off of him.

"Yeah, they been trackin' us," the Marine replied. "Captain had a team punch out to get eyes on."

Kellan was reassured. He just hoped they'd be stepping off soon.

The sound of gunfire erupted around them. Kellan's heart slammed in his chest and his fingers tightened reflexively around the grip of a non-existent M16.

"Contact, nine o'clock," shouted one Marine. M16s and AK-47s continued to chatter. A blast sounded nearby and Kellan looked over at Jonah.

"Grenade," Jonah confirmed Kellan's suspicion.

All around them, Marines scrambled. Kellan could see blurred figures pass by his window. He heard them shouting but couldn't make out words. Their gunner's legs twisted in front of Kellan as the Marine spun his gun in the turret. Kellan just got his ears covered when the Fifty-cal roared. Blistering casings rained down into the Humvee's interior. Kellan and Jonah did their best to avoid them, not wanting a fifty caliber hickey.

Grenades exploded, closer to their position this time. It sounded like more AK-47s firing. M16s chattered close by. Kellan felt impotent. He desperately wanted an M16 so he could step out and join the firefight. He knew it had to be worse for Jonah.

The Fifty-cal roared on the roof of the Humvee again. Expended casings crashed down all around them, bouncing on the metal floor of the victor.

Kellan's door opened abruptly. A uniformed arm reached in and gripped his MTV. Kellan gripped the wrist of his assailant and fought back. He struggled to stay inside the victor.

"I gotta get you to cover, sir," the Marine shouted.

Kellan registered that the cammo diggies were friendly. A quick look at the shoulder told him a Marine Corporal was trying to get him out of the Humvee. A glance behind him told Kellan that Jonah was being extracted as well.

When his boots hit the sand, Kellan ducked and pressed himself to the side of the Humvee. A second Marine fired his weapon around the rear of the victor.

"Wiggins!" The corporal called. The Marine at the rear of the Humvee dropped back to join them. "We're gonna get you and the

First Sergeant to cover inside the house, sir," the Corporal addressed himself to Kellan.

"Keep it simple, call me Kellan," he shouted over the constant weapons fire.

"Armitage," the corporal shouted his own name. Armitage turned his back to Kellan, took Kellan's hand and had him grab the side of Armitage's MTV. "Don't let go. Wiggins will cover our six."

Kellan took a firm grip of each side of Armitage's armor. He felt Wiggins move in close behind. Wiggins reached around Kellan and slapped Armitage in the arm.

"Mounting!" Armitage shouted and stepped around the front of the Humvee.

They stayed in a crouched position, moving as quickly as they could across open ground. Kellan caught glimpses of Marines, all around, firing from behind cover. The large guns on top of the Humvees were roaring.

They burst through a doorway and into a large, open room inside the village's large structure. Wiggins peeled off but Armitage kept moving, leading Kellan farther into the room. Relief swept through Kellan when he saw Jonah already seated on the tiled floor, back to the wall.

Wiggins took up a position by a window and began to fire his weapon. Kellan pulled his sidearm from his leg holster. Beside him, Jonah did the same. Together they each racked a round into the chamber.

More Marines burst through the door, one of them was the Staff Sergeant from their Humvee. "Who cleared the house when you took cover?" he demanded.

"Me and Morgan, Sergeant," shouted one of the Marines.

"Weeks, take Porter, Blaine and Hooks and secure the rest of the house," the Sergeant ordered. "Find a more secure room for our VIPs."

Four Marines detached themselves and moved quickly down the hallway. The four left in the large main room kept up the exchange of fire from the doorway and two windows. Kellan watched the gun battle rage. He hated having to sit it out. Jonah had to be ready to climb the walls.

"Any chance of a sit-rep, Sergeant?" Jonah shouted across the room.

"Looks like an ambush, Top," the Staff Sergeant replied. "The motorcycle was probably a lookout. Large group of heavily armed insurgents came out of nowhere and tried to surround us."

"How're we doin'?" asked Jonah.

The answer was delayed while the Staff Sergeant returned fire. "Captain's out there with the rest of the platoon tryin' to hold them off while this detachment makes sure the two of you make it through okay."

The Marines scrambled as two more of their platoon stumbled through the doorway. One of the newcomers fell heavily to the floor, his uniform showing several dark patches of blood.

Moving as one, Kellan and Jonah crawled forward to the wounded Marine. "We got this, you guys do what you have to." Kellan used a tone of voice he hadn't utilized since his discharge. Finally, he and Jonah could be of some use.

Staying low, they dragged the Marine to the back of the room and out of the way. Jonah grabbed up the discarded M16 and leaned it against the wall within easy reach. Kellan emptied the webbing and pockets of the Marine's uniform. He handed ammunition to Jonah and tore open the IFAK – Individual First Aid Kit – dumping the contents onto the floor.

"Staff Sergeant Mason, we got a room back here with an alcove," a Marine shouted. "It'll provide a little more cover."

"Roger that," the Staff Sergeant, Kellan now knew was named Mason, answered.

"Tell me which room and we'll move there once we're done here," Kellan said, not looking up from his task.

"Fuck, is that Frasier?" someone asked in a worried tone.

Jonah tore open the Marine's MTV to reveal a name patch that read 'Frasier'.

"Get back to your position, Porter," Mason ordered from where he was firing out the front door of the house. "They'll take care of Frasier."

Porter gave brief directions to the secure back bedroom. "Solid copy," Jonah told him.

The largest patches of blood were on the Marine's right arm and leg. "Ka-Bar," Kellan barked.

Jonah retrieved Frasier's knife from the leg sheath and handed it over. Kellan cut open the sleeve and pant leg of Frasier's uniform. The arm wound was the worst. Flesh was devastated and Kellan thought he could see bone fragments in the wound. There was too much damage to apply direct pressure.

"Anybody have a CAT?" Kellan shouted, asking for a Combat Application Tourniquet.

A black strip of fabric hit the tile floor and slid to within Jonah's reach. Kellan took the two-inch thick nylon webbing and slid it over Frasier's arm nearly to his armpit. He twisted the plastic windlass until the blood flow slowed and seemed to cease. Securing the windlass, Kellan shifted to examine the leg wound.

Before Kellan asked, Jonah handed him a thick wad of gauze. Kellan pressed in to the wound on the top of Frazier's thigh. It was a large but clean, circular wound. As he pressed the gauze to that wound, Jonah helped Kellan shift Frasier's leg until they found the jagged exit wound. Jonah handed him another wad of gauze.

"Is there QuikClot?" Kellan asked.

Jonah showed him the packet. "Say when."

When his watch reached ninety seconds, Kellan pulled away the gauze and blood flowed freely. "Now."

Jonah carefully tore open the QuikClot packet and sprinkled the granules into the exit wound. Kellan shifted Frasier's leg so Jonah could sprinkle the QuikClot into the entry wound.

With the bleeding under control, Kellan asked, "Pressure bandage?"

"How's Frasier doing, sir?" Sergeant Mason asked.

"Bleeding's under control," Jonah shouted in answer.

Together, they applied the large cotton pads to the entry and exit wounds. Kellan wrapped the four-inch wide elastic wrap and secured it with the plastic and Velcro fasteners.

"Are you gonna wrap the arm?" Jonah asked.

"Yeah," Kellan replied. "Gauze and triangular bandage?"

Jonah handed over the roll of gauze and Kellan wrapped Frasier's arm. He covered it with the tightly wrapped triangular bandage. The tourniquet would control the bleeding but the bandage would keep the wound as clean as possible.

"He's good for now, Staff Sergeant," Kellan shouted, "but he needs a cas-evac asap!"

"Copy that," replied Mason.

Jonah picked up the M16 and grabbed one side of Frasier's collar. Kellan grabbed the other side as they prepared to move to the more secure room. Two more Marine's fell through the doorway.

"Soames was fragged!" one of the new Marines yelled.

A fresh burst of adrenaline flooding Kellan's system. They left Frasier in the relative safety of the corner and crawled forward. "We'll take care of Soames," Jonah declared.

"Kistler, head back and make sure they've got all the rooms secured back there," Mason ordered sharply.

At first, Kistler didn't move. He stared at Soames, his expression stunned.

"Move it, Kistler!" Mason ordered forcefully.

Kistler jolted. He shook himself visibly and climbed to his feet. Adjusting his weapon, he headed down the hallway toward the back rooms.

"It ain't that bad," Soames said breathlessly, struggling to hide his pain.

"I'll be the judge of that," Kellan replied. He took up Soames' M16 and together, he and Jonah dragged the Marine and lay him next to Frasier.

"Captain says they're holdin' 'em off out there, but it's still gonna be awhile before we can call in a cas-evac," Mason shouted.

Fuck. "Roger that," Kellan answered. If Frasier's arm stayed tourniqueted for too long, he'd likely lose the arm, even if he lived.

Jonah sliced open both legs of Soames' uniform. He was riddled with shrapnel wounds of all levels of severity. "Where does it hurt, Lance Corporal?" Jonah asked.

"My legs and my back," Soames gasped.

They carefully rolled Soames onto his side. Kellan cut his shredded, bloody uniform blouse away from his lower back. "Not too bad," he declared. "Legs are the worst. QuikClot will do the trick."

This time, when they emptied the Marine's pockets, Kellan kept the ammunition and set it with the M16 he'd collected. Jonah retrieved Soames' IFAK and opened the packet of QuikClot. He sprinkled the granules into the shrapnel wounds on the leg closest to him before handing the packet to Kellan. When Kellan finished with Soames' second leg, they rolled him again in order to treat the wounds on his lower back.

"Just relax, Lance Corporal," Kellan said. "We'll get you a cas-evac just as soon as it's clear."

"Prop me up and hand me my weapon," Soames said.

"You get to go hide out in a back room with the rest of the VIPs," Jonah replied.

"Fuck that," Soames groused.

Kellan couldn't help but snort a laugh at Soames' moto. "Staff Sergeant Mason?" Kellan called loudly across the room. "We're pulling back and taking the wounded."

"Roger that," Mason shouted. "Just because you have those M16s, don't think you get to use them."

"Wouldn't dream of it," Jonah replied dryly as he and Kellan grabbed Soames' collar and dragged him down the hall.

"I can walk," Soames protested.

"Shut up," Kellan said, not worried about Marine pride, just wanting to get them all settled in the secure alcove.

Returning to the main room, Kellan checked the ammunition level in the magazine loaded into the second M16. Seeing it was half full, he made sure a round was chambered. He loaded his pockets with spare magazines, picked up the M16 and grabbed Frasier's collar with his other hand.

Reaching the second doorway on the right, they quickly made their way to the small alcove. Soames had managed to gather up some quilts and blankets and started making make-shift beds. He helped them to get Frasier tucked into the rear of the alcove on top of a generous pile of blankets, some folded into a pillow.

"How you doin' for ammo, Marines?" Jonah called as they settled into the alcove next to Soames.

"Okay for now," replied the Marine Kellan thought was named Porter.

"How's it look out there?" asked Jonah.

"They just keep comin', but we're holdin' 'em off," Porter answered. "Captain's still got the worst of it over by the victors."

Kellan tipped his head back against the wall, closed his eyes and listened to the constant burst and blasts of the ongoing gun battle. The sound of exploding grenades was intermittent but never let up. Many of them were close to the outer wall of the room they were in. Kellan wished he had comms so he could get an accurate sit-rep.

"You just *had* to come to Afghanistan, didn't you?" Jonah's annoyed tone was laced with humor.

Kellan grinned, but left his eyes closed. "At least I didn't get myself abducted, this time."

"There's still time, the battle isn't over yet," Jonah replied.

"Maybe you'll be the lucky one this time," Kellan teased.

Jonah snorted. "It would serve you right, having to chase me down across a desert."

Before Kellan could make another witty reply, a grenade blast sounded right outside the wall and the entire room shuddered.

23420

Small arms fire immediately resumed but Kellan thought he heard shouts elsewhere in the house.

"Shit!" Porter swore viciously. "First Sergeant? Staff Sergeant Mason says they took a direct grenade blast up front. They've got wounded and he wants to know if you can help."

Jonah and Kellan were already scrambling to their feet. "Absolutely. Tell Mason we're en route," Jonah answered.

Kellan replaced the ammo magazines in his pockets. Jonah leaned over Frasier and removed the Ka-Bar sheath from his boot and strapped it to his own.

"I'll keep any eye on Frasier," Soames said, handing magazines to Jonah.

Taking up position on either side of the doorway, Kellan and Jonah prepared to make their way back to the front room of the house. The proximity of those last grenade blasts meant insurgents were close enough to possibly make entry, so they needed to be cautious.

Jonah pointed to himself and held up an index finger. He pointed at Kellan and help up two fingers. Kellan acknowledged the order in which they would exit the room.

"Mounting," Jonah shouted, lifted the M16 to his shoulder and stepped out into the hall.

"Mounting," Kellan shouted and followed Jonah out, walking backward as he used his M16 to cover their six.

When Kellan felt Jonah at his back, he knew they had reached the door to the front room.

"It's clear," Jonah said to Kellan, letting him know they were clear to enter the room in relative safety.

"Rodger that," Kellan replied.

"We're coming in, Mason," Jonah shouted, letting the Marine know that friendlies were approaching from their six.

"Come ahead!" Mason yelled over the roar of small weapons fire.

Kellan turned and kneed Jonah in the back, signaling that he was ready to move. Jonah stayed low as they entered the room, sweeping the muzzle of his weapon left to center. Kellan stayed high, sweeping right to center.

There were three Marines down in the center of the room. Kellan crouched and discovered one of them was Corporal Armitage. The other two appeared to have sought cover in the house after they'd been wounded.

Armitage lay on his side. He had multiple shrapnel wounds in the backs of his legs and his buttocks. "I didn't duck quick enough when the grenade made it through the window." Armitage was trying for humor but pain strained his voice.

Kellan patted his arm. "Yeah, well, they *are* quick fuckers." He glanced up at Jonah. "What have you got?"

One of the Marines had shrapnel wounds, but the other had taken a couple of rounds from an AK-47. One of the rounds had nearly obliterated the Marine's calf muscle. It was an ugly and devastating wound.

"Captain Miller has choppers inbound to deal with these fuckers," Mason said, not lifting his cheek from the stock of his weapon.

"Copy that," Kellan responded. That meant things were bad out there and it was a pretty large group of insurgents being held off by a single platoon of Marines.

Working quickly, Jonah and Kellan dragged the wounded Marines to a corner of the room, as secure as possible given the circumstances.

They worked together, with a minimum of words exchanged, patching up the Marines as well as IFAKs would allow.

"Grenade!"

Kellan threw himself over the Marines who lay before him and covered his ears as best he could. The blast made the room shudder and brought dust down all around them. Pushing himself back to his knees, he saw that Jonah had responded the same way.

"Everybody okay?" Jonah shouted toward the front of the room.

"We're good," Mason answered. "It landed outside the wall."

Kellan glanced over his shoulder and saw the bars over the window had sustained some damage in that last blast. The lower corner of one window was twisted and mangled. It indicated just how close of a call that last grenade had been.

Jonah struggled to stem the bleeding in the Marine's devastated lower leg and Kellan scrambled to assist. It seemed to take forever, but finally, between the make-shift tourniquet and direct pressure, they got it under control.

"Grenade!"

Kellan only had enough time to cover one of the wounded Marines with his own body. Almost immediately after the blast, Marines were shouting in alarm.

Pushing up onto his knees, Kellan looked back and saw one of the Marines at the window was now sprawled on the floor. Crawling forward, Kellan checked the wounds and found they were bad. The Marine had taken shrapnel to his face and upper arms.

"They're down one weapon now," Jonah said from beside Kellan.

"I got this," Kellan replied. They'd all be in trouble if the house was overrun by insurgents.

Jonah picked up the discarded M16 and checked its ammunition. He took a knee at the corner of the window, beside where Staff Sergeant Mason was firing out the door of the structure.

"You were determined, weren't you?" Mason asked Jonah, managing to sound amused despite the circumstances.

"Been awhile since I got some," Jonah replied, even as he squeezed off a two round burst.

Kellan dragged the wounded Marine to lay with his other patients and set about opening the IFAK.

"I'm fine, sire," the Marine said through clenched teeth, as he tried to deny that he was in pain.

"Top Carver took up your position," Kellan said as he held direct pressure to the worst of the shrapnel wounds. "How bad is it out there?"

"It's bad, sir," the Marine replied. "Those choppers need to get here quick."

"With Marine pilots, they'll be here before you know it," Kellan reassured himself as much as the young Marine.

"Grenade!"

Kellan didn't get his ears covered in time and the blast left his ears ringing. He shook his head and worked his jaw but nothing helped. It wasn't so bad he couldn't hear the distressed shouts and cries from behind him.

Turning to crawl in the direction of the shouts, Kellan saw two more Marines down.

"Shit! Grenade!"

Kellan dropped to his belly and managed to get his ears covered in time. This blast was danger close. He looked up and was relieved to see that no more Marines were wounded.

"We need more weapons up here," Mason snapped. He keyed his mic to check with his men in the back of the house, but at two per room, they were barely holding on back there.

The Marine whose facial wounds he had just treated suddenly appeared beside him. He kept his wounded arm pressed to his side, but he was mobile and had use of both hands.

"I got this, sir," he said to Kellan. "You go help hold those motherfuckers off us."

Kellan considered his options for several heartbeats. Again, the chances they would all survive were slim, if the insurgents overran the house. With his ears still ringing, Kellan crawled to the second wide window and picked up the discarded M16.

He hadn't felt the recoil of an M16 in seven years but Kellan quickly adjusted. Muscle memory kicked in and he easily began to identify and pick off targets. It wasn't as easy as it had been in '03, the insurgents were better trained and more disciplined than the street fighters had been in Iraq.

"Choppers are three mics out," Mason shouted over the cacophony. "And we got inbound friendlies."

No sooner had Mason said that, than Kellan caught sight of two Marines struggling around a mud brick wall. One of them was obviously wounded, struggling to stay on his feet. His buddy was trying to keep him upright and mobile, at the same time he was trying to cover their six with weapon fire.

Kellan lay down suppressive cover fire. If they could keep the insurgents behind cover, the Marines actually had a shot of making it to the safety of the house.

They were about ten meters out when an insurgent leapt around the brick wall, armed with an AK-47. Kellan targeted him and pulled the trigger twice, sending four rounds into the combatant's body. It was too late, though. A spray of bullets struck the Marines sending them both to the ground in a plume of dust.

"Fuck!" Kellan thought that was Mason. "The choppers are almost here. We gotta get them in here!"

"I'll go."

Kellan almost didn't believe it was Jonah's voice he heard. "The hell you will!" he replied, even as he forced an insurgent back under cover.

"We can't risk Mason, he's the NCOIC for the detachment, and you're not gonna go," Jonah replied quickly.

Before Kellan could further voice his displeasure, Jonah was out the door and running toward the downed Marines. Kellan's heart leapt into his throat. He gripped his weapon tight enough to make his hand ache. The battle itself already had his adrenaline spiked but fear for Jonah's safety made him feel weak and sick.

Kellan forced himself to focus on his task. With is peripheral vision, he monitored Jonah's progress as he made it to the wounded Marines and began to help them struggle to their feet. He could hear the thump of the rotors of the inbound choppers and relief washed over him. But it wasn't over yet.

The bolt of Kellan's M16 slammed back and stayed there. He ejected the expended magazine, letting it fall to the floor. Pulling a fresh one from his back pocket, Kellan slid it home and chambered a round. He looked up in time to see Jonah, sandwiched between the two Marines, stumble and fall to his knees. As big and strong as Jonah was, two wounded Marines were taxing him.

Kellan could see the choppers now. They were small dots in the sky and growing larger by the second.

"Cover me, Mason," Kellan said, positioning himself at the doorway.

"You two don't know the meaning of 'no', do you?" Mason asked.

"Jonah doesn't stumble," Kellan replied. "He needs help."

Before Mason could say anything else, Kellan darted out the door, keeping low and clutching the weapon with both hands. He reached where Jonah was struggling to get the two wounded Marines to their feet. Kellan shouldered the weight of one of them and headed toward the house.

"You're not supposed to be out here!" Jonah shouted, even as he tossed the second Marine over his shoulders.

"You were taking too damn long!" Kellan shot back and took the lead.

The four of them fell through the doorway and onto the floor, right as the choppers passed overhead. The fifty-caliber door guns blended with the low thump of the rotors as the birds made pass after pass over insurgent positions. Kellan took up his position at the window again, but there weren't as many targets now. He was lightheaded with relief, knowing Jonah was back in the safety of the house and unharmed.

Kellan was surprised at the strength of his reaction to Jonah being in danger. They'd been in combat together before and he hadn't reacted like this. Then again, they hadn't had a personal relationship back then.

Mason had a conversation on his comms and to Kellan, it sounded reassuring. The small arms fire had all but ceased and they hadn't seen any movement in several minutes.

"We got corpsmen in bound to our location," Mason said, blowing out a deep, relieved sigh. "The choppers identified an LZ several meters behind us and they're setting down."

That was good. They would be able to load up the worst of the wounded instead of having to wait for a cas-evac.

"First Sergeant Carver? Mr. Reynolds?" Mason called. "Captain Miller says to double time it to the LZ. He wants the two of you out of here and back at the safety of Leatherneck."

Kellan wanted to protest. He felt as though he was abandoning these Marines, but that didn't make sense. Sure, he'd patched a few of them up but the corpsmen would take over now. These weren't his men, they didn't need him. They had their NCOs and their officers.

Jonah was in motion before Kellan. He pulled Kellan to his feet, took the M16 from him and propped it against a wall. With his hand twisted in the shoulder of Kellan's MTV, Jonah turned and shook Mason's hand.

"It was an honor, Staff Sergeant," he said.

"The honor was mine, Top," Mason said solemnly.

Kellan gathered himself and shook Mason's hand as well. "Thank you, Staff Sergeant Mason. For everything."

"Thank you for looking after my men, sir." Mason swallowed hard several times.

"Let's go," Jonah said firmly, tugging Kellan out the door.

Minutes later, as the chopper lifted off to take them back to Camp Leatherneck, Kellan realized his hands were still trembling.

Chapter 9

The day after the gun battle was spent in debrief. It was a battle, like so many other battles that stem from an ambush, except this one involved a non-CIA civilian. No one had done anything wrong. There was nothing that should have been done differently, but Kellan wasn't allowed to go home until the Marine Corps was satisfied with the stories everyone was telling.

Kellan didn't let himself feel exhausted until the wheels of their plane touched down at Ramstein Air Base. Everyone was friendly and accommodating in Germany. They had rooms set aside for Jonah and Kellan, but Kellan didn't plan to spend the night on base. If there were no flights to the states until the next day, Kellan wanted a private room, with private bathing facilities, for the night.

He wanted Jonah and he didn't think that was anyone's business right now.

Someone arranged for a car for them and before he knew it, Kellan and Jonah were checking into the Hotel Merkur. The first thing Kellan wanted was a shower. The facilities at Leatherneck were rudimentary and he'd showered nearly eight hours ago.

Jonah ordered them room service as Kellan washed away the dust of Afghanistan. As the hot water beat down on him, he realized he now had an idea of how Jonah had felt in Iraq, as he'd watched Kellan get dragged away against his will. Luck had been on their side again. Kellan still had Jonah, much to his relief.

When he finished his shower, Kellan picked through the food Jonah had ordered. Jonah went in to shower. Kellan realized he still had to be out of sorts, if he and Jonah were in a hotel room and showering separately.

He retrieved his bag and found the small plastic bottle he had in his dopp kit. It was an airline approved bottle, unlabeled, and appeared to be hair gel. Kellan had packed lubricant just in case; he hadn't expected to have a chance to use it on this trip. Now he was glad he'd been so prepared and optimistic.

Jonah emerged from the bathroom with just a towel around his hips. Kellan thought that was perfect. He was dressed in only a pair of track pants, himself. Not in the mood to fuck around, Kellan walked up to Jonah, wrapped a hand around the nape of his neck and pulled him down for a deep kiss.

After a moment of surprise, Jonah's arms came around Kellan's torso. He moaned into Kellan's mouth.

"What's wrong?" Jonah asked when he pulled back.

Kellan frowned up at him. "We were both in a gun battle two days ago. What do you think is wrong?"

Jonah pulled Kellan close again and kissed him, licking deep into his mouth, his rough palms sending shivers through Kellan's body. Jonah shifted and Kellan's hair was gripped tight in one fist, his cheek cradled in the other.

The look in Jonah's eyes when he broke the kiss sent another shiver through Kellan's body. "That day in Iraq, I wanted you so much. I wanted to be inside you and reassure myself you were okay."

"If it felt anything close to this it must have been hell for you," Kellan whispered. He remembered the way Jonah had watched him that day, stayed close, but never touched. Kellan had been reassured by his mere presence and was simply happy to still be alive.

"It feels that way now. Only this time I can touch you." Jonah emphasized his words by cradling Kellan's face, his thumbs caressing Kellan's cheekbones.

Kellan pressed their mouths together again, making a sloppy mess of it. Their wet lips slid against each other and he liked the desperate feel of it. He tugged on Jonah's towel and it fell away easily.

"Climb up on the bed for me," Kellan whispered against Jonah's swollen mouth. He ran his palms over Jonah's muscled chest, enjoying the feel of the warmth of his skin.

Jonah slid his hands under the waist of Kellan's track pants and gripped his ass firmly. Kellan pushed his hips forward, rubbing his growing erection against Jonah's hip. He moved with Jonah as he backed toward the bed, their mouths never quite fusing as they licked at and tasted one another.

As Jonah climbed up onto the bed, Kellan pushed his pants down over his hips, his hard cock bouncing freely as he kicked them off. He joined Jonah on the bed, pushing him with a hand on his chest until he lay back on the pillows. Kellan crawled between Jonah's thighs and lowered himself so they were chest to chest. "I wanna be inside you so bad," he breathed as he kissed along Jonah's jaw.

"I just wanna be with you, I don't care how." Jonah buried his hand in Kellan's hair and pressed his face Jonah's throat, encouraging the kisses.

Kellan kissed his way down Jonah's chest. He felt the muscles of his stomach clench as he dragged his tongue along their edges. He rose up briefly to snag his small bottle from the bedside table.

"Is that actually lube?" Jonah asked with a soft laugh? "I thought we were going to have to use spit."

"You always said you admired my logistical planning." Kellan smiled down at him, heart threatening to burst from his chest.

Kellan's cock was hard and aching. Part of him wanted to draw this out, take all night. His body just wanted to spill his seed deep inside of Jonah's. Kellan wet his fingers with some lube and slid down between Jonah's open thighs. He circled his fingers around Jonah's tight opening, feeling it clench at his touch. He spread the lube around slowly, slicking Jonah's outer rim. With his other hand, Kellan steadied Jonah's growing erection and placed a kiss on the very tip.

Jonah inhaled sharply, his hips lifting slightly. Kellan wrapped his lips around the reddened head of Jonah's cock and slowly swallowed him down. He kept up the steady circle of his fingers on Jonah's hole, waiting for him relax.

Kellan added lubricant to his fingers and pressed them again to Jonah's hole. He slid his mouth down the length of Jonah's shaft, pushing the flat of his tongue along the thick vein. Jonah's hips flexed and he moaned, his hole clenching rhythmically but the muscle not feeling quite as tight as before.

Kellan pushed against Jonah's hole, working his mouth rapidly up and down Jonah's length. When Jonah's hand rested on the back of his head, Kellan pushed one finger past Jonah's clenching muscles and into his body. Jonah moaned, his hand on Kellan's head clenching convulsively.

Still working his mouth on Jonah's cock, Kellan pushed two fingers into his hole, spreading the lube generously and waiting for the muscles to relax fully. He pulled off of Jonah's erection, circled the head with his tongue, and pushed his mouth down to the base in a smooth motion. Jonah groaned decadently. Around Kellan's fingers, Jonah's body relaxed. It was like Jonah's channel was drawing Kellan's hand inside.

Pulling off, Kellan got to his knees. With trembling hands, he coated his own cock with slick. Propping one hand beside Jonah's head, Kellan used the other to line himself up with Jonah's opening. With all the lube and as relaxed as Jonah was, Kellan slid into Jonah's body easily. One long, easy push of his hips and he was buried all the way inside the tight heat.

Jonah arched up to meet him, fingers digging into the muscles of his back. Jonah's legs came around Kellan's hips, pulling him deeper. He looked up at Kellan, blue eyes luminous and needy. Jonah's heat engulfing Kellan's cock was the final piece. Kellan felt alive and complete.

He groaned, low in his throat, as his skin seemed to tighten on his body. Kellan slid his hands beneath Jonah's back and curled them up over his shoulders. He slid down on top of him, pressing their chests together. Kellan worked his hips in a steady rhythm. Jonah made low, rough sounds with each thrust. Kellan pressed his lips to Jonah's cheek and watched the flush on his cheeks rise. The heat of Jonah's body was intense, it meant Jonah was alive. Jonah was alive and he let Kellan inside of him.

Kellan adjusted his angle slightly, searching for the spot that would bring Jonah off the bed. It took him a few tries, some awkward movements and some affectionate laughter, but he found it. Tendrils of electricity snaked up Kellan's spine as Jonah arched and writhed against him. Kellan reached between their bodies and took Jonah's cock in his hand. He stroked it quickly, aching to feel Jonah come around him.

Jonah's breathing sped up. His body tightened and shuddered. His hand fisted in Kellan's hair again. This time, Kellan's neck arched as his head was pulled back roughly. Jonah buried his face in Kellan's throat, his breath hot against Kellan's skin.

"Come on, baby, come for me," Kellan urged softly, pumping his hips and stroking Jonah quickly.

"Fuck, you feel good inside me, Kel," Jonah whispered harshly.

"Come on, let me feel you," Kellan said. "Show me how alive you are."

That sent Jonah over the edge. His cock pulsed in Kellan's hand, hot come rolling down and over Kellan's fingers. His body tightened around Kellan's cock, gripping him tight. He vibrated violently as he shouted his climax against the skin of Kellan's throat.

That was all Kellan needed. The tight heat and the feel of Jonah against and around him dragged Kellan's climax from him. With a shout, he collapsed down onto Jonah, pulled him close and rode the waves.

"I feel you inside me," Jonah said, arms coming around Kellan's shoulders. "I can feel you coming inside me."

Kellan groaned and swore against the side of Jonah's neck. He trembled violently, his hips thrusting reflexively, sending sparks rocketing from his sensitive cock to scatter inside his skull. Jonah was firm and warm against him, Kellan heard each breath and felt the beat of his heart and knew his was alive.

When Kellan's orgasm released him, he managed to fall just to the side of Jonah. He knew he should pull out and clean them up. He knew he should get them under the covers so they could sleep. He'd do that in just a minute.

Epilogue

The chamber doors were opened and Kellan led their group through into the Senate hearing chambers. There were electronic flashes all around them and a buzz filled the room. Television cameras swiveled to track their passage down the aisle.

Keystone Consulting's General Counsel preceded Kellan to the first seat at the long table. Kellan was seated next. Jonah sat beside Kellan and on the far side, JAS lawyer Mirai Hirata.

Together, they rose to be sworn in before the Senate committee, chaired by Senator Gilchrist.

"For the record, Mr. Reynolds, let's get some things out of the way," Gilchrist said.

"That would be fine, Senator," Kellan responded, prepared for full disclosure.

"This is your last duty as the CEO of Keystone Consulting, correct?" the Senator asked.

"That's correct," Kellan replied into the microphone.

"Why is that?" Gilchrist managed to appear curious despite already knowing the answer.

"I've accepted a position with the Department of Defense."

The Senator nodded and appeared to contemplate Kellan's words. "So, as you give testimony today that implicates the DOD in some unpleasant things, it's safe to say you do not have an ax to grind with them."

"It's very safe to say that, Senator." Kellan laced his fingers together on the table in front of him. He found he was enjoying this little performance they were giving.

"And what position have you accepted?" Gilchrist picked up a pen as if prepared to jot down the title.

Kellan took a breath and leaned into the mic. "Deputy Assistant Secretary of Defense for Special Operations & Combating Terrorism."

"That's a hell of a mouthful." Quiet laughter echoed through the room.

"It is, indeed, Senator. It barely fits on my business cards." Kellan smiled when the laughter renewed.

"And is First Sergeant Carver joining you at the DOD?" Senator Gilchrist gestured at Jonah where he sat stiffly beside Kellan.

"Yes. He will be functioning as one of two military aides." Kellan would also be taking on an officer of the rank of captain or higher, for when it was necessary to interact with the White House or the Joint Chiefs.

"Very well. Now that the formalities are out of the way, let's get started." With several bangs of his gavel, Senator Gilchrist got the hearings underway. "We're here to investigate the matter of Marine Staff Sergeant Miguel Restrepo and the conspiracy to deny him the Medal of Honor, which he unquestionably earned. We will also take testimony regarding the disturbing pattern of veterans of Operations Iraqi Freedom and Enduring Freedom being denied medals on the basis of gender, race and suspected sexual orientation..."

The End

Also by Kendall McKenna

The Recon Diaries
Brothers In Arms
Fire For Effect
The Final Line

Standalone
Waves Break My Fall
A Gentle Kind of Strength
Nights In Canaan

Watch for more at https://www.facebook.com/authorkendallmckenna.